8/2

ROAD TRIP WITH THE BEST MAN

ROAD TRIP WITH THE BEST MAN

SOPHIE PEMBROKE

MILLS & BOON

First published in Great Britain 2018
by Mills & Boon, an imprint of HarperCollins*Publishers*
1 London Bridge Street, London, SE1 9GF

Large Print edition 2018

© 2018 Sophie Pembroke

ISBN: 978-0-263-07429-1

MIX
Paper from
responsible sources
FSC
www.fsc.org   FSC® C007454

This book is produced from independently certified
FSC™ paper to ensure responsible forest management.
For more information visit www.harpercollins.co.uk/green.

Printed and bound in Great Britain
by CPI Group (UK) Ltd, Croydon, CR0 4YY

For everyone who ever wanted to take to the open road and find themselves.

It's never too late.

CHAPTER ONE

DAWN FEATHERINGTON STARED down the aisle at the perfect floral arrangements tied to each row of chairs set out on the grass. The string quartet was playing Pachelbel's *Canon*—again—the officiant smiling serenely at the foot of the pagoda steps. The late-afternoon sun shone down on the manicured lawns of the Californian coastal mansion Justin's mother had insisted would be the perfect venue for the two hundred and fifty guests they needed to invite, lighting up the delicate white ribbons and lace strung around the pagoda.

Everything looked perfect. Until she turned her attention to the expectant guests, all waiting slightly less patiently than they had been twenty minutes ago, and felt her stomach twist.

Because the only thing missing now was the groom.

Dawn ducked back behind the screens that the

venue staff had put in place to keep the bridal party's arrival a secret until the last moment. Behind her, her four sisters whispered amongst themselves, their rose-pink silk bridesmaid dresses rustling with them. She couldn't hear what they were saying, but then she didn't really need to.

Can you believe this is happening again?

No. They were wrong. Justin loved her, he wanted to marry her. He'd hated even having to spend last night in a different hotel—although he'd insisted they had to, for tradition's sake. He'd be here any moment. Probably.

Dawn bit back a sigh. It wasn't as if this exact thing had happened before, anyway—whatever her sisters were whispering. She'd never got *quite* as far as the altar with any of the others. They'd all called it off before it reached this point.

Two broken engagements—one at the rehearsal dinner, but that still wasn't the actual altar, right?—three long-term cohabiting relationships that had never even got as far as the ring and now Justin. Forty minutes late for his own wedding.

It wouldn't be *quite* so bad if every single one of her boyfriends hadn't gone on to marry someone else within twelve to eighteen months. Including, in one particularly soul-destroying case, marrying her own sister.

'The Dry Run.' That was what her sisters called her. Dawn was the woman that guys tried out settling down with before they picked the woman they *actually* wanted to spend the rest of their lives with. And for some reason that woman was never Dawn.

But Justin was different. Wasn't he?

From the moment they'd first met, she'd felt it. She'd been at a work event, one held at an estate not unlike this one, with vineyards stretching back from the gleaming white house. She'd been standing on the terrace, looking out at the sunset, when he'd approached her and made some comment about the hosts that she could barely remember. All she had taken in was his smile and his charm. They'd talked all evening—well, okay, mostly he'd talked, but he had so many interesting things to say! Then, the next day, he'd sent flowers and a note to her office, asking her to meet him at some ridiculously exclusive bar across town.

She went, and the rest was history. They'd announced their engagement four months later and, now, here they were.

Or rather, here *she* was. Justin's whereabouts were still a mystery.

The whispering behind her grew louder and Dawn turned to see the best man, Justin's older brother Cooper, striding across the lawn from the main house towards them. He wasn't smiling. Then again, she hadn't seen him smile yet in the twenty-four hours since they'd met, so that might not actually be a sign.

Dawn sucked in a breath and braced herself.

'He's not coming.' Cooper stood a few feet away, his expression blank. As if he hadn't just torn her whole world apart with three little words.

She'd suspected that Cooper didn't like her since she'd first met him at the rehearsal dinner. But then, he'd never seemed particularly enthusiastic whenever Justin had talked to him on the phone either. And, really, what best man didn't make the effort even to attend the engagement party?

'Way to break it to her gently,' her sister, Marie, said sharply. She wrapped an arm around Dawn's shoulders as their other sisters made sympathetic cooing noises.

Dawn would probably have felt a lot more comforted if Marie hadn't married her ex-boyfriend two years ago.

She could feel all the usual emotions swelling up inside her—the anger, the despair, the gaping emptiness—but she clamped down on them. No. This wasn't going to happen again. It couldn't.

And, if it did, she wasn't going to give any one of her perfect sisters—or Justin's sanctimonious brother—the chance to see it break her.

'Is that for me?' Dawn pointed to the envelope in Cooper's hand, proud of how steady her voice was. Her finger didn't even shake.

She could almost believe she wasn't actually dying on the inside.

Cooper gave a short nod and handed it over—but not, she noticed, before removing a second envelope. One that had his name on it.

Apparently Justin had more to say than just to the bride he'd stood up.

Focusing on keeping her hand steady, she took her letter and untucked the envelope flap. So like Justin, to write an old-fashioned letter. He wasn't the sort to dump a girl by text message— like her second fiancé—or even by email, like boyfriend number three. Justin was a gentleman.

Or he had been, until now.

Inside the envelope she found a single sheet of creamy paper covered in his block print writing —one that Dawn was pretty sure Justin must have taken from the elegant writing desk in his mother's immaculate front room. She scanned the words quickly, then folded it up again and pushed it back into the envelope, making sure not to let her expression change at all.

They were *not* going to win.

'Right. Well, it seems we won't be having a wedding today after all.' Her voice didn't even sound like her own.

'Oh, Dawn!' That was her mother, of course, who'd come to find her father to see what the delay was. 'Oh, not again, honey!'

Dawn kept her gaze fixed on Cooper's face, even as he raised one eyebrow at the word 'again'.

'Will you help me tell the guests?' she asked neutrally.

'I believe that unfortunate task does fall to the best man, traditionally,' Cooper said.

Traditionally. As if this happened at everyone else's weddings, not just hers.

'Great. Okay, then.'

'Do you want me to send them home?' Cooper asked, his voice as bland and unemotional as ever. 'I believe there was a dinner planned...'

And an open bar, actually. That might be important later.

Dawn thought of the tables of canapés and champagne, the four-course meal that Justin's family had insisted on paying for. There wouldn't be any refunds at this point, of course, but it wasn't as though the Edwards family couldn't afford it. And a lot of these people had travelled a long way to be with them on their not-so-special day.

Well, the least she could do was feed them. And give them a good story to tell on the dinner-party circuit.

'No,' she said as firmly as she could manage. 'I'll go tell the venue to get the bar open and prepare to serve dinner. Everyone else should enjoy the day, at least. Excuse me.'

And with that Dawn hitched up her heavy, lace-covered skirt and made for the mansion as fast as she could in her satin heels.

She needed a drink, and a toilet cubicle to hide in, fast.

That way, no one would be able to see her fall apart.

Again.

Cooper watched his brother's jilted bride make her way towards the ridiculously fancy mansion she'd chosen for what was supposed to be her big day. She seemed strangely composed for someone who'd just had their entire future torn away from them.

Which, given the contents of the note Justin had left for him, probably shouldn't have been such a surprise.

I can't go through with it, Cooper. I'm sorry for all the upset this will cause Mother, but I know you'll understand.

You see, this week I've found that I just can't shake the feeling that Dawn has ulterior motives for wanting to marry me. I thought she loved me as much as I loved her. But now I'm worried she loves my money a lot more. I can't face her—not now. I need some time away to think everything through, figure out the truth about our relationship, our feelings.

If I'm wrong I'll make it up to her somehow. But I can't marry her when I'm not one hundred percent sure that it's the right thing to do.

I'm heading up to the beach house for the week to think. I'm sorry to place this on you, brother, but I knew you would be the only one to understand exactly what I'm going through...

Yeah, Cooper understood. Apparently neither Edwards brother was any good at spotting a gold-digger until it was too late.

At least Justin had got out before he reached the altar, which was more than Cooper had managed.

Justin had done the right thing. Even if it kind

of screwed up Cooper's plans for kicking back, getting hammered on high quality whisky and maybe even seducing an attractive guest to help him forget how much he hated weddings. Traditionally, he supposed he should have lined up a bridesmaid, but since they all appeared to be A: married and B: sisters of the bride, he was happy to spurn tradition on this one.

Although maybe his plan, such as it was, wasn't completely ruined—especially since Dawn intended to let the celebratory part of the day go ahead despite not having anything to celebrate.

He just needed to break the news to the dearly beloveds gathered for the non-event.

Couldn't be any harder than facing his father's shareholders after that debacle with Melanie and the Reed takeover, right? Or telling his parents that he'd been conned by the woman he loved and they were all about to get screwed in the divorce courts.

Yeah, this was nothing.

Cooper took a deep breath and walked down the aisle, thankfully alone.

'Ladies and gentlemen, I have some sad news for you all.' Everyone's attention was instantly on him, of course, and Cooper smiled his best reassuring smile. 'I'm afraid that there will not, after all, be a wedding here today.' The expected whispers and groans went up from the crowd. Cooper knew better than to expect real disappointment from any of them. More likely they were mentally preparing their gloating renditions of this story for anyone unfortunate enough not to be there to witness it. Goodness knew there'd been enough stories told about him after his divorce, not all of them even close to the truth.

Not that he cared. What difference did it make to him what people said about him anyway?

But he didn't want them saying that stuff about Justin.

'The bride has requested that you all still stay for dinner, however,' he added, and a more enthusiastic murmur went up at that. 'And I believe the bar will be open imminently.'

Then he stepped out of the way to avoid the stampede.

'Cooper? What's happening? Dawn's parents are in pieces over there, and her sisters...well. Where's Justin?' A dark-haired woman in a too-short pink dress pushed through the crush to get to him. Cooper frowned at her for a moment before recognising her as someone he'd been introduced to at the rehearsal dinner two nights before. Not a bridesmaid, so not one of Dawn's numerous sisters. American, so not Dawn's family, either—apart from her mother's transatlantic twang, they all had the same regional British accent that she did. A friend, then. There hadn't been many of those at the dinner—it had mostly been family. So she had to be... No, he had nothing.

'I'm sorry, have we met?' He smiled his most charming smile, but received only a scowl in return.

'Yes. Last night. I'm Dawn's friend, Ruby.'

'Right. Ruby. Of course.' Yeah, no way was he going to remember that more than a few minutes this time, either. Why waste time on people who weren't going to matter to him in the future? And, since Dawn was no longer going to be his sister-in-law, he didn't need to worry about it.

'So? Where's Justin? Where's Dawn, come to that?'

'Last I saw, Dawn was heading into the venue

to demand they open the bar early,' he replied. 'And Justin… I can't say exactly where he is. But I know he's not coming.' And if for some reason his brother lost his mind and suddenly appeared to try and make up with his bride—if he decided that his love would be enough for both of them, even if Dawn's had never existed—well. Then Cooper would be there to stop him. To keep them apart until Justin came to his senses again and appreciated his lucky escape.

'The bar?' Ruby shook her head, turned on her heel and stalked away from him towards her gold-digging friend—stopping briefly to talk to Dawn's confused parents on her way. Maybe they'd been in on it together, he thought absently. Well, Dawn might not be a heartbroken jilted bride, but if nothing else she had to be bitterly lamenting the loss of all that money. The thought made him smile.

Love, Cooper knew from bitter experience, could make a man act crazy. Justin had done the right thing, and Cooper would make sure he kept doing it.

There was no way he was going to let his little brother make the same awful mistakes he had.

* * *

Dawn had found the perfect hiding spot: in the ladies' room on the second floor, furthest from the bar. There were at least two other bathrooms between there and the ballroom where the not-wedding breakfast would be served, and Dawn couldn't imagine *anyone* traipsing this far away from the complimentary alcohol if they didn't have to.

She was completely alone, just as she needed to be.

'Dawn?'

Completely alone except for Ruby, that was.

'In here,' she said, unlocking the door with a sigh. Ruby, she'd learned over the last couple of years since they'd become friends, never took silence for an answer.

Ruby bustled into the bathroom, slamming the door shut behind her and handing over the bottle of Prosecco she was holding.

'Okay, can someone please explain to me what the *hell* is going on? Because that idiot of a best man was basically useless.'

Reaching into the tiny clutch bag she'd retrieved from her sister Elizabeth on her way back to the mansion, Dawn pulled out the letter from Justin and gave it to Ruby. It wasn't as if *she* needed to read it again, anyway. The words were already burned into her brain.

Dearest Dawn,

I'm so sorry to do this to you, darling, but I know I have to be fair to both of us, to give us both our best chances at a happy future.

I can't be there to marry you today. Please don't ask me why, simply know that when I asked you to be my bride it was because I truly believed that our futures lay together. But the world changes more quickly than we can sometimes imagine.

Cooper will help you with our guests, and explain everything to my parents.

Once again, I'm so sorry, Dawn.

With love and affection,

Justin

Dawn watched as Ruby read the letter, her eyebrows jerking higher with every line. *Yeah, that was my reaction too.* Well, that and her heart cracking in two.

Time to open the Prosecco.

'So, he can't tell you why he didn't show up, he ditched the whole problem onto his idiot brother and still claims he's being *fair* to you?' Ruby sounded incredulous.

'Yes, apparently I have been jilted at the altar for my own good.' Dawn took a swig from the bottle and passed it back to Ruby. 'At least that's an excuse I haven't heard before. I mean, with Richard it was because he realised he wasn't ready to settle down after all—although he did settle down six months later with a redhead he met on his "finding myself" trip around India, incidentally. Harry decided he was gay, after he'd been living with me for three months.'

Ruby stifled a giggle at that. Dawn ignored her and carried on ticking off her disastrous prior relationships on her fingers.

'Patrick left me for a job in Dubai, where he claimed I'd be desperately unhappy so he couldn't ask me to go with him. Ewan cheated on me with his ex-girlfriend and Trevor married my sister instead.'

'Girl, you have the worst luck with men. You should try women instead.'

'Don't think I haven't considered it.' Dawn

sighed. 'I just… I don't understand what's wrong with me.'

'Nothing is wrong with *you,*' Ruby said fiercely. 'Trust me, it's those men who are the fools here.'

'Except every one of them managed to settle down with someone else after they got shot of me,' Dawn pointed out. 'And now Justin… I mean, he just didn't even bother to show up. And he can't tell me why. That's…it's not enough.'

'You need closure,' Ruby said sagely, returning the bottle of Prosecco to her.

Closure. That sounded good. Closing the book on her absurdly cursed love life and moving forward instead. Understanding the mistakes she'd made, or what it was about her that made finding her happy-ever-after so impossible. Because this? This wasn't what all those fairy tales and happy endings had led her to expect from life. And she wanted better for her future.

She wanted to find someone to share her life with. Someone who'd stick by her through the ups and downs, someone to come home to after a hard day at work, someone to *love* her just as she was.

Really, how hard could it be if all four of her sisters had managed it? Not to mention every cousin, friend and family acquaintance she had, except for Ruby. Dawn had attended so many weddings in the last ten years, they'd all started to merge into one.

And now it had been her turn at last and everyone had been so *happy* for her. And relieved, she knew—her family wasn't good at hiding their emotions that way. They'd been relieved that *at last* Dawn was through that terrible run of bad luck and they could all stop worrying about her and get back to being blissfully happy themselves.

Except now it was all ruined.

'Your parents were looking for you,' Ruby said, her voice softer. 'And your sisters. Plus, well, everyone you've ever met.'

Yet Ruby was the only one who'd actually managed to find her. Not that Dawn was particularly surprised by that. Ruby *knew* her—had seen right through her the first day they'd met and declared that they were destined to be best friends. And so they were.

'I don't want to see them.' She loved her family, really she did. And she knew they loved her. But she couldn't take the pity in their eyes one more time. That disappointment and—worse— that sense of inevitability. And she *really* didn't want to hear her mother's, 'Not every woman is meant to be a wife and mother, Dawnie,' speech. Because she *knew* that—of course she did. And if she'd chosen to be alone, to forge her own path through life, that would be great. But she hadn't.

Six times now, she'd thought she'd found true love. She'd thought she'd found forever.

And six times she'd been wrong.

She took another, longer gulp of Prosecco, the bubbles stinging her throat as they went down.

Maybe her mother was right. Maybe it was time to concede defeat. To dedicate her life to being that crazy aunt who was always off on adventures, posting photos of her in exotic places with handsome men she never stayed with long enough for them to let her down.

It wouldn't be a bad life.

'What do you want me to do?' Ruby asked. 'Just say it, and I'll make it happen.'

Ruby, Dawn decided, was the best friend a girl had ever had. Life would be so much easier if she could just fall in love with Ruby. Well, as long as Ruby loved her back, which wasn't at all a sure thing. She wasn't exactly Ruby's type—she preferred blondes who played guitar, if her last three girlfriends were anything to go by. So, no, even Ruby couldn't be her happy-ever-after. Not in a romantic way, anyway.

But she was still the best friend ever.

'I need to get out of here,' Dawn said. 'I need to figure out what happened. What I do next. I don't want anyone to worry about me or anything but I can't stay here. I need to go find… closure.'

Ruby gave a sharp nod. 'Closure it is. Give me five minutes. And finish that bottle while you're waiting.'

CHAPTER TWO

THE PARTY WAS in full swing, the celebratory spirit apparently undimmed by the fact that there hadn't actually been a wedding for them to celebrate. Cooper stayed in the bar long enough to make sure that the venue had everything in hand, then grabbed a bottle of beer from behind the bar and headed out into the darkening evening to find some peace and quiet, his best man duties *done*.

The terrace at the front of the mansion was expansive, elegant and, most importantly to Cooper, empty. Apparently none of the other guests felt inclined to survey the view that Dawn had been *so* taken with that she'd had to book the venue on sight, despite the fact it was convenient for practically nobody. His mother, at least, had seemed pleased with her choice.

Cooper sighed, well aware that the day had turned his already bitter heart just a little more sour.

Even if the wedding *had* gone ahead, he doubted

he'd have been in much of a mood to celebrate today. He'd given his prospective sister-in-law the benefit of the doubt when the save-the-date cards had come out—in fairness, it was unlikely that Justin would have mentioned that the date she'd chosen was the anniversary of Cooper's divorce. Chances were that his brother hadn't even realised or they'd have picked another day. But the fact remained that it was now officially three years since he'd disentangled himself from that messy web of lies and false love and, while his freedom probably *should* be something to be happy about, it seldom felt like it.

But at least his brother hadn't made the same mistake. That was something to celebrate. With a small smile, Cooper raised his beer bottle to the sky and silently toasted Justin's lucky escape.

Then he frowned, peering over the edge of the terrace at the sweeping driveway below. Out there, in the shadows of the swaying trees, he spotted a willowy figure. One in a very distinctive white lace dress.

'Where is she going now?' he murmured to himself as he watched Dawn trip over her train and reach out for the nearest tree to steady herself. Was she drunk?

And, more importantly, was she going after Justin?

Without thinking, Cooper put aside his beer bottle and sprung over the edge of the terrace, landing in a crouch on the packed ground. He strode across the driveway to where was parked the vintage robin's-egg-blue Cadillac convertible he'd hired for Justin to drive away in for his wedding night. It had been his own, personal present to his brother—something far more meaningful than a second toaster, or even the speech he'd written to give to the assembled crowd. The car was a memory that only he and Justin shared. A dream, or a promise, they still had to fulfil.

'When we're grown-ups, we'll be able to do whatever we want,' he remembered saying when Justin had been only seven to his ten. 'We'll get the coolest car ever—'

'A Cadillac?' Justin had interrupted.

'Yeah, a Caddy. And we'll drive it all the way across America together. Just you and me. It'll be the best adventure ever.'

They'd never done it, of course. Life had got

in the way. But renting the car for Justin for this day, the start of the rest of his life, had felt like a reminder never to give up on his dreams, just because he'd been tied down by love, family and the business.

Except now he wasn't, of course. Justin had run and left him to clear up the mess.

Like a drunk woman in a wedding dress trying to break into his incredibly expensive hire car.

'Do you really think you're in any condition to drive that?' Cooper crossed his arms and leant against the far side of the car, glaring over to where Dawn was trying to unlock the driver's side door.

'Do you really think it's your place to try to stop me?' Dawn asked, eyebrows raised. She didn't *sound* drunk, but Cooper was hard pressed to think of another reason she'd be stealing his car.

Yeah, okay, so he was thinking of it as *his*. Since Justin clearly wouldn't be using it for his planned honeymoon road trip with Dawn, it seemed stupid not to make the most of the already paid-for rental. He could take it up the coast, maybe, for a couple of days, until he needed to be back in the office.

Once he'd evicted the woman in white who was trying to steal it.

'Since it's my name on the rental agreement, I think it's exactly my place.' Cooper was gratified to see that his statement at least gave her small pause. 'Where are you planning on taking it, anyway?'

'To find some answers,' Dawn said, her head held high. Her long, pale neck rose elegantly up from the white lace monstrosity of a dress to where her dark hair was curled and braided against the back of her head, tilting her chin up with its weight. She looked every inch the English aristocrat—rather than the low little gold-digger Cooper knew she was.

Her words caught up with him. 'Answers? You mean you're going to find Justin?'

Dawn slammed her hands against the unyielding metal of the car door. 'Of course I am! Did you even read the letter he left for me? Could he have been any more vague? So, yes! Yes, I'm going to go find him, and figure out what the hell happened so I can get my life back on track!'

As it happened, Cooper *had* read the letter—
if only to be sure that his brother wasn't leaving things open for a blissful reunion with his
gold-digging bride. Which meant… 'Except, of
course, Justin didn't tell you where he was going.
Don't you think you should take that as a hint
that he didn't want you chasing after him?'

Dawn's eyes narrowed. 'No, he didn't tell me.
But I'm willing to bet he told *you*. So, spill, Cooper. Where is your brother?'

Damn.

She didn't really expect him to tell her outright,
but maybe she'd get lucky. Maybe there'd be a
clue or something that would lead her to Justin.

Cooper's expression went blank, obviously trying to avoid giving anything away. Dawn sighed.
Still, Justin couldn't have gone far, right? Not
if he'd left those notes for Cooper and her that
morning. Especially since their bags for the honeymoon, according to the carefully planned and
laminated schedule for the day, should be in the
boot of the very car she was trying to unlock.
Stupid vintage cars and their stupid vintage

locks. Why couldn't Cooper have hired them something with central locking, at the very least?

Wait. *Were* the bags in the car? She hadn't checked.

Ignoring Cooper's lack of reply to her question, Dawn hurried around to the boot of the Caddy—trunk, she supposed, since it was an American car—and fiddled with the key Ruby had pinched from Cooper's bag for her until the boot popped open.

Empty.

The boot, trunk, whatever you wanted to call it, was empty.

'Where're my bags?' she asked in a whisper.

Cooper followed her round to stand beside her, and they stared at the lack of suitcases together. 'There should be bags?'

'Yes!' Dawn could feel the desperation leaking out in her voice. 'We packed all the bags for our honeymoon and put them in Justin's car yesterday.' They'd had a late lunch together back at Justin's hotel before Dawn had headed off to spend the night with her sisters at their hotel across town. Justin had been a staunch believer in the 'bad luck for the groom to see the bride before the wedding' thing and, quite honestly, Dawn hadn't wanted to tempt fate either. Which seemed doubly stupid now. 'He was supposed to transfer them to *this* car this morning. I figured he'd have at least left mine when he dropped off those bloody letters earlier.'

'He didn't.'

'Well, I can see that!' Dawn's voice was getting high and squeaky now, and she didn't even care.

'No, I mean he didn't bring the letters here. I found them both this morning—they'd been slipped under my hotel room door in one envelope, with my name on it. I thought they were the notes for my speech I'd asked my secretary to drop over and just shoved them in my jacket pocket. I only checked them once we realised that Justin still wasn't here...'

'So he never even came here this morning,' Dawn said softly. 'So all my things...they're still in his car. Which is probably wherever he is.'

Her clothes. Her ridiculously expensive wedding-night lingerie. Her toiletries. Her honeymoon reading. Her *passport*. All she had with her here was a tiny clutch bag with some face powder, a dull nude lipstick she'd never wear in every-day life, a spare pair of stockings, her phone and her credit card, in case there was a problem with the open bar at the venue. Even last night she'd borrowed things from her sisters and had worn the 'Mrs Edwards' pyjamas they'd bought her—which she hoped they burned as soon as they got back to the hotel.

She had *nothing*. Not even a husband.

'I'm sure your family can—'

'No!' Dawn cut him off before he could even *suggest* she crawl back to her family, broken and in need of help. Again.

She'd done that too often in the past. This time, she needed to fix things herself.

Yes, she had nothing. Yes, this was basically the worst she'd ever felt in her whole life.

But that just meant that things could only get better from here on. Right?

At least, they would if she *made* them better. If she took charge of her life for once and stopped waiting for a happy-ever-after to save her.

'Okay, I need you to tell me where Justin is,' she said as calmly as reasonably as possible. 'He has my belongings. My passport was in his travel wallet with his, ready for our honeymoon. If he's not going to marry me, then I need to check out my visa, figure out what I do next, and in order to achieve that I need my stuff.' And she needed closure. She needed Justin to look her in the eye and tell her what had gone wrong. What had changed since lunch time yesterday that had made him run?

She needed him to tell her what was wrong with her so she could *fix* it and bloody well make her own happily ever after, with or without a man.

But, somehow, she suspected Cooper would react better to the more practical approach.

'Look,' she said when he hesitated. 'You want me out of your brother's life, right? I mean, that much has been obvious since you called to not congratulate us on our engagement.' *Are you sure about this?* was what he'd actually said. *Isn't it a bit fast?*

She had no idea where that instant dislike for her had come from, but Justin had told her he was like that with any girl he got serious about, so she was willing to bet it was more of a Cooper problem than a Dawn one.

'It's not what *I* want that matters,' Cooper said. He left the fact that Justin obviously wanted her out of his life unsaid, which was possibly the nicest thing he'd ever done for her.

'My point is, it's quite hard for me to, say, up and leave the country to start over somewhere else while Justin has my passport.' Never mind that she had no intention of leaving the States if she didn't have to, especially since it would involve her traipsing back to Britain and her parents with her tail between her legs. If Cooper needed to believe that she was on her way out of Justin's life to tell her where he was, then he could believe that.

He didn't need to know that her passport wasn't the only thing Dawn wanted from Justin. The answers she needed were none of his business.

Cooper sighed, his broad shoulders sinking slightly as he realised she wasn't going to give up. Dawn stood firm, staring him down, not giving him a second to rethink that realisation.

'Listen, Dawn, Justin said in his note that he needed to get away, he needed time to think. To refocus himself, he said. He needs to be away from *everyone* right now—family, friends and especially you. You need to give him that time.'

'Time to think,' Dawn echoed, a thought of her own crystallising in her brain.

'Exactly.' Cooper sounded relieved. He shouldn't. 'Why don't you spend some time with your family, while they're over here, try and relax too? I mean, this must have all been very stressful for you.' The disbelief was strong in his voice on that last point, but it didn't matter. He'd already told Dawn what she needed to know.

There was only one place Justin went when he needed to get away from everything and think. He'd told her on their third date at that hot new restaurant that served everything with kale.

She knew where she needed to go.

'I could do that,' she said agreeably. 'Or I could head over to your family's beach house in the Hamptons and find Justin.'

Cooper's eyes widened, just enough for her to know she'd guessed right.

'I think I know which I'd rather do, don't you?' Dawn smiled triumphantly and enjoyed seeing Cooper's face fall.

At least she'd come out on top *once* today.

* * *

'I didn't say he was at the beach house,' Cooper said as soon as he gathered his wits again. How could she possibly know that? He felt in his pocket to make sure the letter Justin had written him was still there. He wouldn't have put it past Dawn to have pickpocketed it from his jacket when they were investigating the trunk of the Caddy. She'd obviously already stolen the car keys from his bag, so thievery wasn't beyond her. Not to mention the millions of dollars she had hoped to take his brother for.

Dawn slammed the trunk closed. 'You didn't have to. I know my... I know Justin.'

For a moment there, Cooper almost thought he heard sadness in her voice as she failed to find a word to describe his brother in relation to her. He wasn't her husband, that was for sure. And she couldn't possibly still think of him as her fiancé, or even boyfriend, now, could she?

Except he had a very bad feeling that if Dawn went to the beach house to find him she'd go out of her way to convince Justin to be exactly that once again. That was what a gold-digger would do, right? She'd invested too much time and energy in Justin as a prospect to give up now. She'd probably even try and talk him into eloping to Vegas and making things official as soon as she had her passport back.

Her passport. She didn't have her passport. And she wasn't a US citizen or a permanent resident, so she would need it to fly across the country to the Hamptons where Justin was holed up.

He would have flown, Cooper realised. Anything else would have been crazy. Which meant he'd probably already be there, and Dawn's belongings were in some long-stay car park at the airport, locked in his car. Even if she had the keys, she'd have to hunt through several thousands of cars to find his. But that, he suspected, wouldn't stop Dawn from heading to New York State to find Justin.

'Even if he is at the beach house—and I'm not saying he is,' he added quickly, off Dawn's smug smile. 'Say he is there. How, exactly, are you planning on joining him, given that he has your passport?'

That wiped that smile off her face. But only for a moment.

Grinning widely, she held up the keys to the Caddy. 'I'll drive.'

Since she hadn't been able actually to open the door a few minutes ago, Cooper doubted that she was capable of driving forty-eight straight hours or so across the entire continental US, but the determined gleam in her eye still gave him pause.

'Really. You, all on your own. Across the whole of America. Alone.'

'If I have to,' Dawn said stubbornly. 'If that's the only way to get to Justin, yes.'

Yeah, this wasn't about her passport at all, was it? She wasn't setting off on this absurd road trip to get her stuff and hightail it back to Britain.

She was doing this to get Justin back. And he simply could not allow that.

'Give me the keys.' He held a hand out across the bonnet.

'No!'

'The car is hired in my name,' he said patiently. 'If I call and report it stolen, the cops will have caught up to you before you even get out of the state. Besides, how much have you had to drink?'

'Not much,' she mumbled, sounding less certain. 'Fine, then I'll hire another car.'

'With what proof of ID?'

'I'll take my dad's rental.' She was getting desperate now, he could tell. And that was bad. Desperate people did desperate things.

'No,' he said, making what might possibly be the worst decision of his life. 'We'll take this car. Now, give me the keys.'

'We?' Dawn asked, dropping the keys into his open palm.

Cooper crossed to the driver's side and unlocked the car.

'We,' he confirmed. 'And I'm driving.'

CHAPTER THREE

DAWN WOKE UP as they drove through what she thought must be San Francisco.

They.

She and Cooper.

How the hell had that happened?

She kept her eyes closed, so Cooper wouldn't know she was awake, while she tried to figure it all out.

It might be Ruby's fault. These sorts of things—crazy, unpredictable, ridiculous things—usually were. If she hadn't forced that Prosecco on her then Dawn would have been clear-headed enough not to get into this position. Possibly. Okay, fine, but at least she'd have been able to open the car door the first time and drive *herself* away from her nightmare of a not-wedding.

Of course, if Cooper hadn't intervened, she wouldn't have known where she was going, and who knew how long it would have taken her to figure out that Justin had run off with her passport and suitcase?

Justin.

Of course. It was *Justin's* fault. All of it.

She felt a little better for deciding that, so risked opening her eyes.

'Sobered up yet?' Cooper asked without looking at her. 'There are some painkillers in the glove box.'

'I had, like, *two* glasses of Prosecco, Cooper.' Even if they hadn't actually been in a glass. And probably not as good as the champagne Mrs Edwards had ordered to go with the wedding breakfast her guests would be sitting down to eat around now. 'I wasn't drunk.' Was that the only reason he'd insisted on driving her? Because he thought she was too drunk to do it herself?

Cooper sighed. 'Well, there goes the only justification I could come up with for this crazy road trip.'

'What's crazy about it?' Shifting in her seat, Dawn tried to get comfortable and work out the kink in her neck from sleeping with her head against the window. How long had they been on the road, anyway? If the bright lights around them really were San Francisco, it must have been about an hour since they'd left the venue.

'Everything,' Cooper said flatly.

Dawn ignored him. Clearly he didn't understand about closure. He didn't understand her. And that was fine—why should he? In a day or so she'd have what she needed and he'd be out of her life for good. Right?

Wait. Frowning, Dawn tried to pull up a mental image of the map of the USA she'd had on her wall as a teenager, when she'd planned to escape the stifling perfection of her family and run away to her mother's homeland, the States, as soon as she was old enough.

She couldn't exactly remember *all* the particulars of the interstates and roads, but she did remember one crucial thing: America was big.

Really big.

And the Hamptons were right on the other side of it from where she'd planned to get married today.

She shuffled around in the leather passenger seat of the Caddy again, trying to get her skirt into something resembling a comfortable position. American cars might be bigger and arguably better than the rest, but *no* car was truly comfy when wearing several thousand dollars' worth of lace and silk. The voluminous skirt would have looked wonderful walking down the aisle, or dancing the first dance, but Dawn felt it was rather wasted being crammed into the front seat of what was clearly Cooper's dream car.

'How far exactly is it to the beach house, any-way?' she asked as nonchalantly as she could. However far it was, it was where she needed to go.

But she had a nagging feeling it might take a little longer than the day or so she'd imagined when she'd suggested driving there.

'About three thousand miles,' Cooper replied, equally casually. 'Give or take.'

'Three thousand miles.' Dawn swallowed. Hard.

'Give or take,' Cooper repeated. 'About forty-eight hours of solid driving, mostly along Inter-state 80.'

'You've done this before?' That was good. If he'd driven this way before, then it was clearly doable and not quite as insane as it sounded in her head.

'Never,' Cooper said, and Dawn's spirits sank again. 'Justin and I always planned to do a coast-to-coast road trip one day, though. Had it all planned out and everything. We were going to do it over a couple of weeks one summer. Hire a vintage Caddy like this one, really make the most of it.'

And instead he was making the trip with her—his sister-in-law who wasn't. Dawn wanted to ask why he and Justin had never taken their trip, but the closed expression on Cooper's face stopped her.

Well, that, and the phrases 'a couple of weeks' and 'forty-eight hours of solid driving' echoing around her head.

'We're going to need to stop overnight, then,' she said.

'Over *several* nights,' Cooper corrected. 'Even if we split the driving, we'll both need to rest. Plus this car is a classic, vintage model. It's been refurbished, of course, but still. It's not exactly covered for non-stop cross-country travel.'

'How many days do you think it will take us?' Dawn asked, staring at the hard planes of his face, the set jaw. Two days ago, she'd never even met this man. Yesterday she'd realised he seriously disliked her. And now it looked as though they were going to be spending an awful lot of time together.

Maybe this wasn't the best idea she'd ever had.

Cooper shrugged, never taking his eyes off the road. 'Maybe four or five. If we really push it.'

And longer if they didn't. Possibly a lot longer if anything went wrong with the car.

Dawn tried to remember how much space she had left on her credit card. Motel rooms for a week were going to add up fast. Not to mention food, petrol and everything else. She forced herself to take deep breaths and stay calm. The last thing she needed was Cooper figuring out how much she was freaking out.

She just had to stick to the plan. Get to the Hamptons, get her stuff back and find the closure she needed to move on. After that, this whole trip would just be a memory—like a half-remembered, crazy dream.

One more breath, and she felt the calm settling over her again. That was better.

Then she looked down at the puddle of lace

and silk she was sitting in and cursed Justin one more time for good measure.

'In that case, I'm really going to need to find some new clothes.'

'It's not too late to turn back, you know.' Cooper could tell she was getting cold feet. She was British—what did she know about great American road trips? Or how *long* they took? For some reason, tourists always seemed to underestimate the size of this country. And he could totally use that to his advantage now. 'I mean, we're only an hour or so out. It would be no big thing at all to turn round, head back to that lovely mansion you picked and get back to your regularly scheduled life. You can tell your family you just needed to get some space, so you went for a drive. No one's going to think anything's odd about that, not after the day you've had.'

Cooper did his best to sound sympathetic, rather than gleeful. He might have always wanted to do a big coast-to-coast road trip, but this wasn't exactly how he'd pictured it—even if the car was perfect. No, the best thing for everyone involved was for Dawn to give up now and go home.

'In fact, we're still going to be closer to the wedding venue than to the beach house for another....' he glanced down at the dashboard '—one thousand, four hundred and seventy miles. I mean, we haven't even crossed the bridge to Oakland yet. Perfect time to turn round.'

'No.' Just the one word, but Cooper could hear a world of stubbornness behind it.

'You know, I could call Justin and ask him to courier your passport and stuff to you,' he pointed out, entirely reasonably, in his opinion.

'Still no.'

Damn. He must have laid it on a bit thick. He'd been so sure she'd been about ready to back down from this crazy stunt. What was she really hoping to achieve? To prove to Justin how much she truly loved him so he'd forget that, until she drove across the country, he knew she'd only wanted to marry him for his money? Did she really think that would work?

Cooper sighed. The worst part was, she might be right. After all, if *he* wasn't afraid Justin might fall for the big romantic gesture, he wouldn't be turning onto Interstate 80 at the San Francisco-to-Oakland bridge right now.

The problem was that Justin had always been the romantic one—even if he'd been the only one to see through Rachel the one time Cooper had let down his walls long enough to fall in love. Justin still believed in love and happy-ever-afters in a way that Cooper never had—and certainly hadn't since he'd learned the hard way that the only thing other people wanted from him was his money and influence.

But Justin... Justin had always been easily swayed by a beautiful woman—just like their father. And Dawn was, Cooper could admit, objectively speaking a beautiful woman. With that dark hair and pale skin, not to mention those bright green eyes...

Of course, every woman looked beautiful on her wedding day. Which was no doubt the reason Dawn had decided to chase after Justin in her wedding dress and full make-up—to make maximum impact.

Cooper smiled to himself. At least he could be pretty certain that the dress and make-up would look rather less impressive in a week's time, when they finally reached the Hamptons and Justin. And, since he was the one who knew where they were going, he'd have to do his best to make sure that any new clothes she did manage to get her hands on wouldn't be half as alluring.

'You know, I've always wanted to take a proper road trip too.' Cooper glanced over and saw that Dawn had kicked off her shiny satin high heels and rested her feet against the dashboard. Her perfectly painted toenails peeked out from under the edge of her wedding dress, glossy red.

He looked away. 'Have you really?' As of five minutes ago, he'd bet.

'Absolutely,' Dawn said, nodding enthusiastically. 'And really, there just isn't enough of Britain to count as a *proper* road trip. You can drive the whole thing in a day or so. No, you have to come to the States for a real road trip experience like this.'

'And what constitutes a "real road trip experience" in your mind?' Cooper asked sceptically.

'Uh, well…snacks, obviously. And music. You need a soundtrack.' She looked dubiously at the ancient radio the Caddy boasted. Cooper suspected that if it picked up anything it would be radio waves beamed straight from the fifties, giving them a steady diet of Elvis and Buddy Holly. The car's engine and working parts had all been updated enough that he trusted the Caddy to make the distance he needed, but the interior and aesthetics were most definitely of its time—radio included.

'What else?' he pressed.

'Stopping to eat in diners—like, proper, authentic American ones, with pancakes and burgers and stuff.'

'Are you hungry, by any chance?' Cooper asked. 'Because that's the second food item on your essentials list so far. And you've only come up with three things.'

'Kooky roadside attractions!' Dawn shouted. 'That's what a road trip needs! I mean, that's what I've always imagined for my dream road trip.'

That she'd clearly come up with five minutes ago as a way of convincing him she was going through with this. Right. 'Roadside attractions,' he repeated dubiously.

'Yeah, you know—like the world's biggest ball of twine. That sort of thing.'

'The world's largest ball of twine is in Kansas,' Cooper replied automatically, and regretted it almost instantly. 'We're not going through Kansas.'

Dawn stared at him. He tried to pretend he hadn't noticed. 'How do you even know that?'

He shrugged. 'I know things.' Such as the world's largest ball of twine made by one person was in Minnesota, which they also weren't going through. But he wasn't telling her that.

'You like kooky roadside attractions too!' Dawn declared. 'Well, this is perfect, then. We can bond over them on our road trip.'

She sounded so pleased with herself for figuring out something about him that Cooper had to pour cold water on her optimism.

'Not much point in bonding though, really, is there?' he pointed out. 'Not when you'll be out of my life, and my brother's life, the moment you get your passport back. Right?'

Because that was the deal here. He wasn't helping her win Justin back. He was making sure she never even had the chance to try.

And, the sooner she accepted that, the better.

* * *

'Right.' Dawn dropped her feet from the dashboard and shoved them back into the stupid, uncomfortable wedding shoes her sister had insisted she buy.

For a moment there, she'd let herself get carried away with the trip. With the escape. Running away was so appealing right now...but she wasn't. She was running towards something.

Justin.

Not to win him back, exactly, whatever Cooper thought. But to figure out the truth.

She had to remember what she was in this for: closure. Not kooky roadside attractions.

Well, maybe one or two. They *did* have to take breaks, after all.

Speaking of which...

'Do you think we could stop somewhere soon?' she asked. 'Not to turn around or go back or anything. But you were right. I *am* hungry.'

Breakfast and mimosas had been hours and hours ago, and she hadn't been able to stomach lunch, when the ceremony was supposed to start at two. All she'd had since Justin's nonappearance was half a bottle of Prosecco, a couple of canapés and a breath mint—all courtesy of Ruby.

Cooper made an impatient noise in the back of his throat. 'We can stop when we get to Sacramento.'

'Sacramento?' Dawn didn't want to admit that she had no idea where that was but…she really had no idea where that was.

'It's only another hour or so from here,' Cooper told her.

Dawn wondered if her stomach might start to eat itself before then.

'So, you know this route pretty well, then?' she asked, more to distract herself from her growling stomach than anything else.

'It's mostly one road,' Cooper answered. 'Just follow the I-80 to New Jersey, and from there I'm practically home.'

'Right. You live in New York.' Too far to consider flying over to meet his brother's girlfriend in California, of course.

'When I'm in the country.' And too busy to bother anyway. Even if he worked for the same family company as Justin, somehow Cooper managed to make it more all-consuming.

What was it Justin had always said about his brother? *'He doesn't need love, he has work. It's basically the same thing for him.'*

How sad that must be. Sure, Dawn was all for job satisfaction—that was what had brought her out to the States in the first place. Her company had needed someone to take over the marketing of one of their products on this side of the Atlantic, and they wanted someone who understood the true Britishness of it, as well as how to sell it to the locals. With her American mother and very British father, Dawn had been perfectly positioned for the job.

But a job wasn't a life. It was something to do in between the more meaningful parts—the parts of a life that involved other people. Relationships, family, friendships, love.

The part of her life that had used to be all about Justin until that afternoon.

Suddenly her job was looking a lot more appealing.

'So, what is it you love so much about your job?' she asked. Maybe she could learn something from Cooper. Such as how to forget all about the more painful aspects of her existence for a while.

'You mean apart from the money?' Cooper asked drily.

Dawn raised her eyebrows as she looked at him. 'Given it's your family business, I'm pretty sure you'd still have plenty of money even if you didn't work yourself half to death.' The Edwards family had made the rich list every year for the last hundred, after all.

'Who says I work myself that hard?'

'Your brother.'

A muscle jumped in his jaw at her statement, but he didn't respond.

'So I figure, if you're working that hard it has to be for more that money. So is it love of the job? The challenge of it all? Or…?' Another option occurred to her. One far more fitting to her own situation. 'Or is it an escape?'

Because that would explain it. But what was he trying to escape from?

'You know, it's funny. My brother never told me all that much about you at all. Whirlwind romance, was it?'

Dawn looked away at his obvious attempt to

turn the questioning round on her. 'I wouldn't say "whirlwind".'

They'd been together over three months before Justin had proposed. That wasn't whirlwind, was it?

'And a short engagement too.' He glanced away from the road to raise an eyebrow at her.

'Well, my work secondment was almost over, and if I wanted to stay, well, we had to make some decisions quickly.'

'I'm sure. Of course, I know my mother was scandalised at having to try and plan a whole wedding in so short a time.'

'We were lucky her name opened a lot of doors when it came to finding a venue,' Dawn admitted.

'You mean her money.'

'Both, probably.' Of course, that had also meant that Mrs Edwards had had the first and final say on where they held the wedding, what it looked like and who they invited.

'Hmm.'

Dawn frowned. 'Is there something you're not asking me? I mean, something you want to know?' Because it felt very much like he was skirting around some accusation she couldn't quite grasp. 'Wait—did you think we *had* to get married? You know, for…old-fashioned reasons?' The kind of reason that would have had her father on Justin's doorstep demanding he marry his daughter now he'd ruined her.

'You mean, did I think you were pregnant? No.' Cooper's words were blunt, unemotional, but the image they brought up stung Dawn's heart all the same.

She'd imagined it, even if he hadn't. Her life with Justin. A family of her own. All of it.

And now it was never, ever going to happen.

Turning in her seat, Dawn stared out of the window at the lights and landscape rushing past. San Francisco Bay stretched out under them as they crossed the road bridge back to the mainland, on the interstate at last. The road that would take them all the way across the country. All the way to Justin and closure.

'You might as well try and sleep some more,' Cooper said suddenly. 'I'll stop in Sacramento so we can eat. Then it's your turn to drive.'

Her turn. Right.

'You're sure you don't just want me to drop

you off somewhere so you can fly home?' she asked. 'I promise I'll look after the stupid car.'

But Cooper shook his head. 'No. We're in this together now.'

'Why?' Who in their right mind would want to take this trip with her?

'I have my reasons.' And obviously no interest in sharing them with her.

Dawn sighed and rested her head against the window again. If she needed to drive on the interstate, she really should try to sleep.

Besides, apparently she had plenty more days ahead of her to figure out exactly what Cooper was getting out of this crazy road trip.

CHAPTER FOUR

AT LEAST SHE didn't snore. Cooper supposed that he should be grateful for small mercies, given the current situation. The car was running fine, the interstate was as clear as it ever was and Dawn didn't snore. She did, however, sleep all the way to Sacramento, a full hour and a half's drive. Not that he was complaining. He was a long-time fan of his own company and rather less keen on hers.

As the road swung towards the north of Sacramento's centre, Cooper kept an eye out for any decent looking place to grab a coffee and maybe something to eat. He'd promised Dawn, after all, and besides, his own stomach had started to remind him that it was a long time since lunch—and there hadn't been much of that, anyway. He'd been saving himself for the wedding breakfast—not expecting to be on the road by the time everyone else sat down to eat it.

Spotting some familiar lit-up signs, he signalled to leave the interstate and pulled into a parking lot shortly after. The retail park wasn't huge, but it had both chain restaurants and stores. Since he hadn't exactly packed for this trip either, he could do with picking up a few things—and getting the hell out of the tux his mother had insisted he wear. Suits were one thing—Cooper could appreciate the value of a good suit. But bow ties were simply never going to be his style.

He glanced across at his companion and the wide lace skirts covering every inch of the passenger seat. At least he had to be more comfortable than she was. And that corset style top looked actually painful.

Yeah, they should stop and change. If nothing else, pulling up at a motel with a bride in a few hours' time was just going to look tacky.

'Dawn?' he said softly, then repeated it louder when she didn't stir. 'Dawn.'

Her eyes flickered open. 'Are we there?'

'We're in Sacramento,' he said, unsure if she was awake enough even to know where she was asking if they were. 'Come on. We can pick up some supplies and get something to eat before we carry on.'

She nodded, but her eyes were fluttering closed again. Cooper rolled his eyes and climbed out of the car, slamming the door loudly behind him.

That woke her up.

He locked up then took off towards the nearest store that looked as though it would stock everything they needed for the next few days. When he reached the door, he glanced back and saw Dawn struggling to catch him up, her wedding dress tangling around her legs and hampering her movements.

'Honeymoon over already, huh?' an older guy asked, stacking carts by the door.

Cooper ignored him. Yeah, they really needed to get some different clothes.

Inside, the harsh overhead lighting turned Dawn's lace dress almost a pale yellow, but they were still getting plenty of stares from the other shoppers.

'Let's split up,' he suggested. The whole bridal thing was making him uncomfortable, and she wasn't even *his* bride. 'It'll be quicker.'

Dawn nodded her agreement. 'Fine. I saw

signs for the bathrooms at the front of the store, so I can get out of this dress too.' She looked almost as happy as him at the prospect. 'Where shall I meet you?'

'The burger joint across the way?' Cooper had a sudden, unusual hankering for a proper burger and the place looked big enough that they should be able to seat them, even if it was busy. 'Whoever gets done first can get us a table.'

'Works for me,' Dawn said, shrugging as she headed off towards the women's clothes.

Cooper moved around the shop quickly and efficiently. Years of business travel—and the occasional lost suitcase—meant he knew exactly what he needed to survive a few nights on the road, and at least this time he didn't need to replace any of his suits. A couple of pairs of jeans, some tee shirts, a slightly thicker zip-up top, underwear, socks, sneakers and essential toiletries, and he was done. They might not be of his usual quality or brand, but they'd do for a few days. He headed to the tills to pay, then straight to the restroom to change, hoping they'd at least be clean.

He felt better just for being in casual clothes.

With autumn still a few weeks off, it was definitely *far* too hot for a tuxedo in California. And if he had to take this stupid road trip, he at least wanted to be comfortable doing it.

Pushing open the door, he headed back out to the front of the store, planning to stash his discarded clothes and the rest of his new purchases in the car before heading across to check out the burger bar menu. But when he stepped out into the small corridor outside the restrooms, he found Dawn waiting for him—still in her wedding dress.

'Let me guess,' he said, drily. 'You neglected to pack your wallet and now you need money from me.' How predictable. But Dawn wouldn't be the first woman to use him as her personal ATM, and as long as it meant that she couldn't worm her way into the family's finances longer term he was willing to live with it. Especially as even he knew that wedding dresses didn't have pockets.

But Dawn blinked at him with confusion, then held up a bag of clearly already paid-for shopping. 'I had my credit card in my clutch bag. I just can't undo this dress on my own.'

Oh. *Oh.* 'You need my help.'

'Please.' She looked pained just to have to ask him, but she turned and presented her back to him all the same. 'If you could just loosen the corset ties enough, I should be able to wriggle out of it myself.'

As she spoke, the doors to the main store opened again and two large men walked through, their curious eyes fixing instantly on Dawn and her wedding dress.

Cooper scanned the doors leading off the small corridor. He was *not* undressing a woman in public, with an audience to boot.

'In here,' he said, giving her a gentle push towards the baby-change room and hoping it wasn't already occupied by a squalling infant with a dirty diaper.

Fortunately, it was free. Cooper locked the door behind them before addressing the issue of Dawn's gown.

'How did you even get into this thing?' he asked as he fumbled with the corset laces at the back of the dress.

'I had help,' she said drily. 'Lots of help.'

'Your bridesmaids?' How could a dress possibly be as complicated as this? There must be a better way of getting her out of it. What if he pulled on that end of the lace? Would that make it better or—?

'Ow!' Dawn cried as the dress tightened around her middle.

Right. Worse.

'Yes, my bridesmaids,' she went on as Cooper quickly went back to loosening the laces the slow and boring way. 'My four sisters, all of whom had their own wedding day experiences to draw on to tell me *exactly* how I was supposed to do things.'

She didn't sound particularly pleased about that, Cooper noticed.

Finally, the last of the laces gave way and the wedding dress parted at the top, leaving the long, graceful curve of Dawn's back uncovered. No bra with the strapless dress, he realised. Cooper found himself staring at the expanse of bare skin, his fingers still gripping the edges of the dress, wondering if she was wearing anything at all under the wedding gown...

Dawn glanced back over her shoulder at him,

her green eyes wide and innocent as she held the top of the dress tight against her chest.

Cooper blinked and stumbled back. What was he doing?

'Right, you're out,' he said, reversing towards the door at speed. 'I'll, uh, wait for you outside.'

'Thanks.' Dawn gave him a grateful smile—one without any hint of come-on or desire in it—and he cursed himself again for his most inappropriate thoughts. 'But why don't I meet you over at the restaurant like we planned? This might take me a few minutes.'

'Right. Stick to the plan.' Cooper unlocked the door and slipped through it without opening it too far, to try and preserve Dawn's modesty.

Then, once he heard her lock it again from the inside, he strode away as fast as he could towards the burger bar across the parking lot. It was Dawn's turn to drive next. Maybe a beer would help him erase the image of his brother's fiancée's skin and the unexpected urge he'd felt to touch it.

Dawn let out a long breath as she locked the baby-change room door and heard Cooper's footsteps rushing away. For a moment there, she'd seen something in his eyes she couldn't quite identify but, whatever it was, it had caused him to tense up completely.

She sighed. They had a long way to go on this road trip. She couldn't afford awkwardness between them.

Still, getting out of the damn wedding dress would help. It wasn't even as if the lace and silk concoction was one *she'd* chosen. Her gown had been picked by committee—the only dress out of the hundreds she'd tried on that she, her mother, Justin's mother and all her sisters could agree on.

And now it was just another reminder of this most terrible day.

Dropping the dress from where she held it against her bare breasts, Dawn shoved the fabric down over her hips and stepped out of it, suddenly feeling free again. With a smile, she dressed quickly in the new underwear, denim skirt and pink tee shirt she'd bought—cheap, cheerful and easy to wash and wear again. She'd picked up a pair of white sneakers too, along with extra undies, a couple of other thin tee shirts and a sweater for if the evenings grew cooler. None of it had cost much individually, but all together it made her even more nervous about the price of motel rooms on the road and the remaining credit left on her card.

Next, she pulled out the pack of cleansing wipes she'd bought and set about removing every trace of the make-up her sister Beatrice had carefully applied that morning. Normally, Dawn wouldn't have expected it to last so long but, given the trowel Bea appeared to have applied it with, maybe she wasn't so surprised.

'You want it to stay in place all through the photos, Dawnie. Just leave this to me.'

Finally, after removing forty-eight hair grips—Dawn had counted—she pulled out the new hairbrush from the bag and began brushing out the artful curls and braids her other sister, Jennifer, had insisted on. Then she tied it back into a simple ponytail to keep it out of her way, finally feeling like herself again.

She shoved everything else back into the bag her purchases had come in—all except the wedding dress, which was too huge and unwieldy to fit. She'd have to lug it over to the restaurant as it was.

Unless she didn't.

Dawn eyed the rubbish bin in the corner of the room. It was obviously designed for nappies and other baby-related rubbish, but it was larger than she'd have expected. Maybe even large enough for a ridiculous quantity of silk and lace.

She hesitated, biting down on her lip as she held the wedding gown against her. She shouldn't. It was a horrendous waste of money and crafts-manship, and even sentiment.

But, on the other hand, the dress was a stark reminder that *nothing* about her wedding day had gone to plan. From the preparations being railroaded by her family and Justin's mother, to Justin not actually *showing up*, why on earth would she want to keep the dress as a reminder of the day she *hadn't* got married?

So, she shouldn't. But she was going to.

Biting back a gleeful grin, Dawn crammed her wedding dress into the bin and pressed the lid down on top. Then, feeling a hundred pounds lighter, she grabbed her shopping bag and un-locked the door, striding out to begin her life over again.

Starting with dinner with her non-brother-in-law, and ending when she finally looked Justin in the eye and understood why he'd jilted her at the altar.

After that? All bets were off.

Cooper had secured a table near the window, so he could watch for Dawn crossing the parking lot to join him, but in the end she still took him by surprise.

As a petite, fresh-faced young woman slid into the booth seat opposite him, her dark ponytail bobbing cheerfully, he opened his mouth to tell her that he was waiting for someone—before he realised it was Dawn.

He snapped his jaw closed again and stared.

'What looks good here?' Dawn asked, her attention already on the menu, rather than him.

But Cooper's gaze was fixed on her unfamiliar face.

When he'd first seen her, dressed in a tailored dress that showed off her figure, and a matching jacket that he knew his mother would approve of, he'd known her type instantly. The glossy, carefully waved hair, the perfect make-up, the nude heels... She was the sort of woman he'd dated for years, the sort of woman he'd *married,* come to that. She'd even looked a little like Rachel, now he thought about it.

Maybe that was why he'd been suspicious of her from the start.

But now, with her face scrubbed clean until her cheeks shone pink, her hair pulled back from her face and wearing a short denim skirt, pale pink tee and sneakers…she looked like a different person.

One far too young to be marrying his brother. Or conning him out of his fortune, for that matter.

Which was probably why she'd got as far as she had, of course. Justin wasn't an idiot. He'd have spotted a gold-digger a mile off if she'd been obvious about it.

Suddenly, his brother's last-minute revelation and flight made more sense to Cooper.

'Do you have your UK driver's licence with you?' he asked, ignoring her question about the food.

Dawn frowned at him over the top of the menu. 'Actually, yes. I keep it in my phone case. Why?'

'Because I'm not sure you look old enough to

drive in that outfit, and if we get pulled over I want to know how much trouble we're in.'

Her face cleared at his words and she laughed—high, bright and far happier than he'd expect from a woman who'd just been jilted by the love of her life.

'That's why I have it,' she admitted. 'I've been ID'd so often in bars since I arrived in this country, and I couldn't face being turned away from the bar at my own wedding.'

'How old are you, anyway?' he asked, suddenly curious. He knew so little about this woman who had almost been his sister-in-law. And, looking at her now, he wondered how much of the stuff he *did* know was an act, an attempt to be the sort of bride Justin would expect.

'Twenty-eight,' she said promptly. 'And, yes, I know, I look younger. I'm actually the third-eldest of my sisters.'

'How many of you are there?' He had a vague image of a gaggle of women all wearing the same pink bridesmaid dresses, but he hadn't actually stopped long enough to count them.

'Five, including me.'

'So you're right in the middle.'

'That's right.' Dawn's smile was too tight, which made him question what part of this conversation she felt uncomfortable about. Her entire family had flown out for the wedding, so she couldn't be embarrassed by them. Could she?

'You don't get on with your sisters?' he asked, probing the obvious wound. If he was stuck travelling with Dawn for the next handful of days he might as well use the time wisely, learning as much about her as possible, to help keep Justin safe from any attempts on her part to win him back.

'Oh, no. I love my sisters.' Dawn didn't sound entirely convinced by her own words.

'But?'

She gave him a weak smile. 'You know siblings. They always think they know what's best for you.'

'Most of the time, I've found that they do.' He thought back to Justin's comments about Rachel the week before Cooper had married her.

'Are you sure it's the real thing, Coop? That she's in love with you, *not just the idea of being part of the Edwards legacy?'*

And here he was, playing exactly the same part

for Justin. He just hoped he could do a better job of it. That Justin would believe him, even though Cooper hadn't believed his brother last time.

That still rankled, he knew. Cooper's lack of faith in Justin had caused a gulf between them that neither brother seemed to know how to cross. But maybe now, having lived the same experience, they would find their way back to each other again. Cooper hoped so.

He'd never blamed Justin for what had happened with Rachel, only himself. The same way he'd never blamed his mother for introducing him to Melanie and asking him to mentor her as she learned the ropes of the company.

His mother couldn't have known that wasn't all her beautiful young friend was hoping to learn, and Cooper had been so inexperienced and keen to show off his place in the company that it hadn't even occurred to him that Melanie might have ulterior motives. That she was less interested in *him* than his knowledge of company secrets. Or that she'd use everything he showed her and take it back to her boyfriend's rival company—leaving Cooper to deal with his furious father and desperately trying to rebuild trust with the board.

Which only made the whole situation with Rachel more galling. Having been taken in once, he'd thought he was too cynical, too knowing, to fall for the same tricks again. Until Rachel had swept into his life, blinding him with her polish and beauty. Suddenly he was spending his fortune on keeping her in jewellery and designer clothes, on being seen in the right places and with the right people. And Justin was the only one who'd called him on it.

Time to return the favour.

'Come on,' he said, lifting the menu again and studying it. 'We need to get a move on if we're going to make it to Reno before we stop for the night.'

The sooner they made it across the country, the sooner he could help Justin extricate himself from his gold-digger fiancée—for good.

CHAPTER FIVE

DAWN HADN'T DRIVEN much since her arrival in America—but she was damned if she was going to let Cooper know that. This was *her* road trip he was gate-crashing, so *of course* she was going to drive most of it. On the right side of the road and everything. She just needed Cooper to add her to the insurance first. One quick phone call and she was good to go.

At least, now she was no longer weighed down by her wedding dress, driving wasn't the impossibility it would have been before. So all she had to do was figure out the controls and dashboard of the vintage Cadillac and try not to crash into anything between Sacramento and Reno. How hard could that be?

Cooper gave her a quick primer on the car as she started the engine, and she nodded as if it all made perfect sense. She'd figure it out once she got on the road, she was sure.

'And I just stick on the I-80?' she asked, wanting confirmation of the route in case he fell asleep while she drove. It seemed kind of ridiculous that one road could take them all the way across the country, but Cooper nodded.

'Until we hit New Jersey later in the week, pretty much. Although we'll probably want to turn off into Reno to find somewhere to stay tonight.'

'Right, then.' The car jerked into motion, juddering out of the parking space Cooper had chosen. Dawn was glad she didn't have to reverse the ridiculously long car just yet. Getting it to go forward was tricky enough.

'You'll get used to it,' Cooper told her, stretching out his legs as best as he could in the passenger seat, his arms folded across his broad chest. He might look less formal in jeans and a tee shirt, but somehow Dawn couldn't help but feel he was no less intimidating. 'Just need to gentle her along.'

His eyes fell closed as the car jumped forward again. He couldn't really be planning to sleep, could he?

He'd been quiet over dinner, barely even contributing to the conversation after his questions about her sisters. She'd kept up a constant chatter to start with, uncomfortable with his silence, but there were only so many observations she could make about the restaurant, the menu and the food before she ran out of things to say.

At least, things that weren't to do with her abysmal love life, or questions about Cooper's own life that she knew without asking he would never answer.

Justin, she remembered, had told her everything there was to know about himself on their first date. Everything he thought mattered, anyway. He was an open book, he'd said, and she'd loved reading him. Loved learning all his quirks and ticks. What he liked, what he didn't. How he felt—about the world, about his life, about her.

She remembered the first party he'd taken her to as his date—one held at a business partner's property down in southern California. She'd felt so out of place in her usual party dress, which suddenly seemed a little drab and simple next to the designer outfits of the other women present. And then she'd managed to put her foot in it hugely when a stranger had asked how she liked the wine and she admitted it was a little sharp for her—only to learn that the man asking was, in fact, the vintner. By the end of the night she'd been miserable and desperate to go home, sure that Justin had to be regretting ever inviting her. But Justin had simply smiled, kissed her and told her that she'd know what not to do next time. Then, the next day, he'd made her an appointment at a dress shop in town so she could buy something more appropriate to wear for the party he wanted her to join him at that weekend.

It had just been so easy to fall into sync with him because he didn't hide anything away. His expectations, feelings and opinions were always on show. Dawn had never had to guess with Justin.

But he'd never talked much about his brother. Which was a shame, because she couldn't help but feel that understanding Cooper better would make the next few days go a lot smoother. Even though Justin had spoken at length about his childhood, his parents and his friends, Cooper had hardly ever even come up in conversation. Why had she never noticed that before?

She let her gaze drift over to the elder Edwards brother, still prone in the passenger seat, taking in the parts of him that felt familiar. His nose was ruler-straight, just like Justin's, and his dark hair the same colour. But there were so many differences, too: Cooper was taller, broader and his jawline much harder. But with his eyes closed she couldn't see the biggest difference between the brothers—the dark, harsh, bitterness she always saw in Cooper's eyes.

What had caused that? And, whatever it was, did it explain why he'd agreed to drive across the country with her to find Justin?

What did he think she was going to do when she got there that she needed a chaperone?

Shaking her head, Dawn frowned down at the steering wheel, took a deep breath and prepared to try again. Really, this was no different from when her father had taught her to drive over ten years ago. She just needed to practise. Practice, her mother had always told her, made perfect.

Which didn't explain why, after all her practice at relationships, another man had walked off and left her. Again.

But she wasn't thinking about that. She was thinking about the open road and the future.

'Are you planning on leaving the parking lot at any time tonight?' Cooper asked without opening his eyes.

Setting her jaw, Dawn pressed down the accelerator and began to drive.

Her future was waiting, after all.

'Cooper? I'm guessing this is Reno?'

Dawn's words jerked him awake—which was the first sign that he'd fallen asleep in the first place. He hadn't expected to, given the way the car had been lurching around as Dawn got used to driving it, but apparently she must be a fast learner, because he didn't remember much of anything after they'd left Sacramento.

He opened his eyes in time to see the Reno arch lit up almost overhead, announcing that they had arrived at 'the biggest little city in the world'.

'You wanted to stop here tonight, right?' Dawn asked, glancing away from the road for a second to look at him. Then her gaze was fixed back on the traffic in front of them, her hands, pale in the light from the illuminations overhead, gripping the steering wheel tightly. If she'd been doing that for the full two hours since he'd fallen asleep, they must be aching by now. No wonder she was ready to stop for the night.

'Yeah,' he said, peering out of the window at the lit-up hotel and casino signs they passed. She must have pulled off the interstate and into the city while he was still asleep—another sign that she really needed to stop driving. He'd intended to spend some of the drive on his phone, finding them a hotel for the night, but since they were already here they might as well go and knock on reception desks until they found somewhere suitable. 'We'll find somewhere safe to park this thing, then hunt down a couple of rooms for the night.' The last thing he needed was someone stealing their hired Caddy before they'd even got any further than Nevada.

He'd never spent much time in Reno before, and he didn't intend to spend much time here now. Neither he nor Dawn were there for the gambling or the entertainment—it was just another stop on a journey he hadn't fully intended to make. They'd find a hotel, get some sleep and be on the road again first thing. But as he strode along the lively streets—lit up with music, illuminated signs and chatter—Cooper realised that Dawn was no longer beside him.

'Dawn?' He spun round, trying to spot her in the crowds. It was nearly eleven at night, but the streets of Reno were still packed with people. Had she given him the slip? Cooper swore as he realised that she was still in possession of the keys to the Caddy. She could be racing off towards Justin, alone, right now. Maybe she'd been faking her tiredness, her need to stop for the night, just to lull him into a false sense of security so she could ditch him.

'Sorry!' Dawn popped up beside him, his racing heart jumping at her sudden re-appearance. 'I got distracted by one of the bars—they had a band playing and, well, I'm a sucker for live music. It's been forever since I saw a band live! Justin was never really interested. Sorry again,' she added, frowning at him as he realised he hadn't responded.

He'd been so sure she had gone.

Why *hadn't* she gone?

Cooper would have done. Why risk being tied down to him, the one person who could reasonably be expected to stop her from convincing

Justin that she loved him and that they should still get married, when she had a chance to go it alone?

'Cooper?' Dawn's frown deepened. She reached out and touched his hand, and the feel of her fingers against his skin jerked him out of his reverie.

'I think I saw a suitable hotel down this way,' he said, waving vaguely in the direction of a side street. 'You should stick close.'

'Right. Will do.' Dawn gave him a sharp nod and stayed right by his side as he led her towards the lights of what thankfully turned out to be a halfway decent hotel. Even better, it had two free rooms left, right next to each other, and Cooper took them without even checking with Dawn, handing over his credit card happily as the slot machines of the casino downstairs rang out merrily, signalling that someone had just won big.

What did it matter if the hotel wasn't as luxurious as he'd normally expect—or as she had obviously hoped to grow accustomed to by marrying Justin? They'd be on their way first thing anyway.

He handed Dawn her key card and she bit down on her lower lip as she took it.

'I can pay for my own room, you know,' she said. 'I'm not expecting you to foot the bill for this whole road trip or anything.'

Ah. So *that* was how she was going to play it. Suddenly, it all made sense.

Dawn was going to use this trip together to get him on her side. To convince him that she truly did love Justin, not just his money. Starting by offering to pay her own way.

It was a decent plan, he had to admit. If Justin hadn't already told Cooper about her gold-digging ways, maybe he'd even have fallen for it.

Although, given his history with Rachel, probably not. Even she'd gone Dutch on dinner at the start—but it had only lasted until he'd fallen for her and started insisting on paying for everything out of love. She'd stopped offering after that—and from there it had been only a small step to demanding presents to prove his love.

The fact Dawn thought she could manipulate him like that, the way Rachel had, made his shoulders tense.

'You can pay tomorrow night,' he said coldly as he turned and headed for the lifts. 'I'll see you back here at eight-thirty. Sharp.'

And with that he left her alone in the lobby with her bag, even though her room would be right next to his. He didn't want her getting the wrong idea about this trip, after all.

The last thing he wanted was Dawn thinking that the two of them could become *friends*.

This was *not* how Dawn had expected to be spending her wedding night.

Letting the hotel room door swing shut behind her, Dawn leant against it and surveyed the small double bed, the tiny fridge in the corner and the TV on the wall. The window looking out over the street was ajar and she could hear the noise and laughter of downtown Reno filtering up through it.

Not exactly the four-poster bed in the luxury boutique hotel on the Californian coast that she'd booked for her and Justin's first night as man and wife.

Dropping her carrier bag of meagre belongings on the floor, she pulled her phone out of her pocket and stared at the screen. No missed calls. No messages. No voicemails.

No word from Justin at all, except that infernal note he'd left her.

Dawn tossed the phone onto the bed and sank down to the floor, wrapping her arms around her knees. She was exhausted, but she knew she wouldn't sleep, even if the hotel bed wasn't as uncomfortable and the blankets as scratchy as they looked.

What was she doing? Racing across the country to try and find something to make herself feel better? To restore her broken confidence?

After picking herself up and starting again so many times before, when was she going to accept that this just wasn't the life she was supposed to lead? She should have known better than even to try again after the last time, and the time before that.

And *Justin.* Gorgeous, rich, successful, *happy* Justin. How could she have imagined for a second that he could really stay that happy spending the rest of his life with her?

She'd tried so hard to fit in with his lifestyle, to be the sort of woman he'd be proud to have on his arm. She'd filled her wardrobe with those neat but expensive shift dresses he liked her in and binned all her old jeans, especially the ones with the holes in the knees. She'd stopped scraping her hair back and started spending time actually styling it in the mornings, wearing more make-up than a brush of powder and some lip balm when she remembered, or brightly coloured lipsticks when she wanted to make an impact.

She'd favoured neutrals over colours, even though they made her feel washed out and bland, because he'd told her that his mother believed that bright colours on a woman looked trashy. She'd read up on things he was interested in and learned to understand the markets and investments well enough to follow conversations at dinners in fancy restaurants. Hell, she'd even gone skiing with him and his friends, running up her credit-card balance even more to buy all the required equipment for the week, despite the fact that she hated the cold and had never skied before.

She'd given him her all. And it hadn't been enough.

She wasn't enough.

Sighing, Dawn pushed herself up off the floor

and rummaged in the carrier bag for the new toothbrush and toothpaste she'd bought when they'd stopped. She hadn't wanted to waste any of her remaining dollars on non-essentials, so there wasn't much else in the bag, but at least she'd thought to pick up a cheap charger for her phone.

Now, when Justin didn't call, she'd know it was because he didn't want to speak to her and not because she'd run out of battery. *Yay.*

Okay, she wasn't going to think about him any more. Not tonight, anyway. She was going to wash, get changed and get into bed. She needed her sleep if Cooper wanted her to drive again the next morning.

Of course, as soon as she'd finished cleaning her teeth and stripped off her skirt and tee shirt, she realised the thing she'd forgotten to buy at the shop.

Pyjamas.

'Damn it.' Frustration taking over, she threw her bag towards the bed, missing and sending the bedside lamp crashing to the floor as the ceramic base smashed. The light fizzed and went out, and she stared at it in the semi-darkness, the room only lit now by the illuminated signs outside her window.

Her anger drained away. She'd have to pay for that. Literally. With money she barely had.

This whole thing was a mistake.

'Dawn?' The banging on the door accompanying her name snapped her out of her reverie. 'Are you okay in there?'

Cooper. Of course—his room was right next door. God only knew what he thought she was doing in there.

'Fine!' she called back, kneeling to gather the pieces of the lamp. 'Sorry, just knocked something over. Nothing to worry about!' Her voice was too high, too desperate, and he obviously heard it.

'Open the door, Dawn,' he said after a moment.

Sighing, she pulled on her pink tee shirt again, hoping it was long enough to cover at least the top of her legs. She might not know Cooper well yet, but she knew enough to be certain he wasn't going away until she opened the door.

'I broke the lamp, that's all,' she said, pulling the door wide to show him. He hadn't changed yet, she noticed, so was still wearing his jeans and tee shirt, making her feel woefully under-dressed. 'I'll pay for it myself when we check out.'

She watched as his gaze took in the darkened room, the lopsided lampshade then, very briefly, her bare legs. Clearing his throat, he stared at her face instead.

'You're not hurt?' he asked.

She shook her head. 'Just been a very long day.'

Cooper gave a short nod. 'Get some sleep. I'll see you in the morning.'

And he was gone, leaving Dawn alone with her broken lamp and her imaginings of what might have been if Justin had only showed up that afternoon.

CHAPTER SIX

SOMEHOW, COOPER FELT more tired the next morning than he had when he'd fallen into the lumpy hotel bed the night before. Ideal for a long day of driving, really.

He'd like to blame the poor-quality mattress, or the noise from the casino below, or even the tiny bottle of rum he'd liberated from the minibar before he'd fallen into bed. But, if he was honest with himself, he knew *exactly* what had kept him awake the night before.

Dawn Featherington.

Not the woman herself, of course—there'd been no sound from her room after the almighty crash that had had him worrying she'd thrown herself though the window without opening it. His heart had raced as he'd stormed out of his room and into hers, only to find her pink-cheeked and embarrassed but unhurt. At least, physically.

She hadn't been able to hide the tear tracks on her cheeks, though, or the redness around her eyes. Her long, bare legs might have distracted him for a second—really, who wouldn't have been distracted by those?—but mostly he'd seen her distress, even in the poorly lit room.

And he knew, absolutely, that it had nothing to do with a broken lamp.

Ever since he'd read Justin's note, he'd been assuming that Dawn was just like Rachel. His ex-wife had set the bar for unfeeling, manipulative gold-diggers, but after seeing Dawn last night he was sure there was something more to this story.

Maybe it was just the frustration of seeing all her efforts come to nothing when Justin hadn't shown up for the wedding. But Cooper couldn't help but feel he was missing something about her. *Could* she really have loved him?

Groaning, Cooper rolled out of bed and prepared to meet Dawn down in the lobby. At least he had another few days on the road to figure out what he was going to do when they finally caught up with Justin.

A shower and a change of clothes helped him

feel a lot more human, and seeing Dawn waiting for him by the reception desk, looking through leaflets for local attractions, relaxed him a little too. He hadn't really expected her to run off on her own this time, but there was always the chance. He didn't want her going after Justin alone. Not until he was sure about her motives.

She was wearing the same skirt she'd bought yesterday with a bright, sunny yellow tee shirt this time—one that didn't look as if it would cover *any* of her legs. Not that he was thinking about her legs. Much.

Engaged to your brother, Coop, he reminded himself. *Also probably after the family money. Forget the legs.*

'Ready to go?' he asked, lifting his own bag as she turned around. 'We can grab breakfast on the road.'

She nodded, shoving a couple of leaflets into her plastic bag as she picked it up.

'I spoke with Reception about the lamp,' she said as they stepped out into the sunlight. 'Gave them my credit card details.'

'They probably have breakages like that all the time. I wouldn't worry.' Although she clearly was, for some reason. Some reason he suspected that was bigger than just a broken lamp.

And it was up to him to figure out what it was. To understand this woman before they reached the Hamptons.

Good job he had plenty of time and an enclosed space to do it in, otherwise he'd have been screwed. Understanding people, and their motives, had never been his strong suit. As evidenced by his marriage, if nothing else.

They stopped at a coffee shop to grab to-go cups and doughnuts before heading back to the car.

'It's going to be a hot one today.' Dawn stared up at the bright blue sky as he opened the door. 'Shame the Caddy was built before air-conditioning became an automatic add-on.'

'The Caddy is a *classic*,' Cooper said, instantly defensive. 'Besides, it's a convertible. No need for air-con. Not when you have the wind in your hair.'

'And bugs in your teeth,' Dawn muttered.

Cooper ignored her. *Clearly* this Brit couldn't understand classic American design.

He took the first shift behind the wheel, wishing that the car had cup holders, instead of him needing to hold his coffee between his thighs. Not that he'd mention that disappointment to Dawn, of course. She had too little respect for the car as it was.

'You should name her,' Dawn said as he pulled back onto the interstate minutes later.

'Name who?' he asked, not taking his eyes off the road.

'The car. Since you love her so.' There was a forced sort of jolliness to her voice, and Cooper wondered if she was trying to put the previous night behind her.

'I don't name cars,' he said flatly.

'Well, maybe you could start.'

They drove in silence for a while, the only noise the rustle of the doughnut bag. Until, just as he finished the last of his coffee, Dawn spoke again.

'Cassandra,' she said. 'Cassie for short.'

'You're actually naming the car.'

'Well, you weren't going to.'

'Not Cassie.' That wasn't…regal enough for a car like this.

'Calliope.'

'No.'

'Carly?'

'Definitely not.' She glanced over as he shuddered at the suggestion. 'High school ex-girlfriend,' he explained.

'Ah. Not Carly, then.'

She was quiet for so long that he thought she might have actually given up on the idea.

Until she said, 'Claudia.'

Cooper considered. Then, against his better judgement, he smiled.

'Claudia it is.'

A new day. A new start. A new Dawn, even.

That was what Dawn had been telling herself since she'd woken up. It was no longer her wedding day. Which meant that the rest of her life started now.

Even if she was going to spend almost the first week of it on a road trip with her almost-husband's brother.

She'd picked her sunniest yellow tee shirt, plucked up all her courage to speak to the reception staff about the broken lamp and accepted that breakfast was going to comprise mainly of sugar and caffeine. Hell, she'd even persuaded Cooper to lighten up enough to name the car.

Claudia was an *excellent* name, although she still maintained there was nothing wrong with Cassandra, either.

The only problem was, that kind of cheeriness took effort. It meant constantly distracting herself from everything she'd lost.

And Cooper wasn't helping with that.

She tried to start all sorts of diverting conversations—about cities he'd travelled to, his work, his family—but got nowhere. Somehow, Cooper managed to answer even the most open-ended of questions with a definitive yes, no or sometimes just a grunt. What was it with this man and small talk?

She even reached for the radio once or twice, but Cooper's glare put her off the idea. Apparently he *really* wasn't a morning person.

Justin hadn't been either, so maybe it was a family thing. Whenever they'd gone away together, he'd objected to her getting up at the break of dawn, ready to explore. In his mind, weekends and holidays were for sleeping late, then staying out later that night. Dawn, on the other hand, hated wasting so much of the day. Still, since they hadn't lived together, and Justin didn't like week-night sleepovers, it wasn't as if it had been a problem every day. Dawn had managed to adjust to his schedule, more or less, whenever they'd stayed out of town together. And, when she couldn't, she'd just used her quiet, alone morning time to read up on fun places they could go and explore when Justin *did* get up. Or if she ever came back alone, if he had other plans for the day.

She frowned to herself at the memory. Why had they always had to do what *Justin* wanted, anyway?

Maybe it was time to start demanding she get to do what *she* wanted for a change. Starting with this road trip.

'So, where shall we stop next?' she asked Cooper, after they'd been on the road for a couple of hours. Sugar for breakfast really wasn't her thing, and she was aching for some savoury food, even if lunchtime realistically was still more than an hour away.

But Cooper just shrugged, forgoing anything even approaching an answer this time.

'I thought you had this route all mapped out.' Dawn reached under her seat for the road atlas she'd found the day before. It was old, but she could always double-check the details with the travel app on her phone.

'I wasn't exactly planning on taking this trip, remember?' Cooper said, not even glancing her way.

'Well, neither was I, buddy,' Dawn grumbled under her breath. 'You can thank your brother for that one.'

That did earn her a look, but one she couldn't quite read.

'I guess I just figured you'd done all the planning for when you meant to take the road trip with Justin,' she said. Although, if he hadn't, that meant she could start choosing some of their stops. She could insist they went where *she* wanted to stop. It was strangely liberating.

Then she frowned again, as another question occurred to her. 'Why *didn't* you take that road trip?'

'I got married that summer instead.' Cooper's words were even, unemotional, but Dawn could tell there was a whole big, messy story behind them. One that would definitely distract her from thinking about Justin—if she could get him to tell it.

'I didn't know you'd ever been married.' In fact, it was hard to imagine Cooper stopping glowering long enough for anyone to fall in love with him, but she didn't mention that.

'It didn't take,' he said flatly. But Dawn saw the way he glanced down at his left hand, as if he were still expecting to see a wedding band there.

'Justin never said.' Which was strange, although not unimaginable. Justin had always shied away from the subject of Cooper. Maybe this was why. 'Can I ask what happened?'

'No.'

'Right.' Of course not. 'I just thought—'

Cooper interrupted her with an exasperated sigh. 'Would you like to spend the next thousand miles or so discussing possible reasons Justin might have had for not turning up to marry you yesterday?'

'I suppose not,' Dawn admitted. Although, in some ways, that was *exactly* what she wanted to do. Just not with Cooper. What she really needed was Ruby, a bottle or two of wine, a bowl of potato wedges with sour cream and sweet chilli sauce and several uninterrupted hours to dissect exactly what had gone wrong in her relationship.

Justin's brother was no substitute for that.

And none of it changed the fact that the only person who could give her the actual answers she needed was Justin himself. Who was still— she did some quick mental arithmetic—forty-one driving hours away.

Yeah, she was definitely going to need to stop for lunch before then. But at least she got to choose where.

Leaning forward, Dawn rooted around in her bag for the leaflets she'd picked up at the hotel, fanning them out as she looked for a likely place to stop and eat. If Cooper wasn't going to distract her, she'd occupy herself by planning their journey. Her way.

Checking their location on her phone, and matching it up with the ancient road atlas she'd found in the glove box, she narrowed down her choices, putting some leaflets aside for later in the trip. Eventually, she held up one with the picture of a giant polar bear on the front.

'Elko, Nevada,' she said triumphantly.

'Excuse me?'

'That's where we should stop for lunch,' Dawn explained. 'Elko, Nevada. Home of the world's largest dead polar bear.' It was spontaneous, quirky and all the things she hadn't been lately. Totally out of character, really. Except…it didn't feel that way. It felt as if maybe this *could* be her character, if she let it.

As though this was the Dawn she'd been looking for.

'Why would we want to eat lunch with a dead polar bear?' Cooper asked, eyebrows raised. 'And besides, I thought we decided that we weren't stopping for kitsch roadside attractions on this trip.'

'We have to eat some time,' Dawn said reasonably. 'Why not take a peek at White King while we're at it?'

'White King?'

'That's the polar bear's name.'

Cooper sighed. 'Of course the polar bear has a name.'

'You're the one who named the car Claudia,' Dawn said with a shrug.

'I didn't—' Cooper bit off whatever argument he was about to make, and Dawn hid her grin. Baiting Cooper was far more fun than learning about his secret marriage, anyway. 'Fine. How far is Elko?'

Dawn bounced a little in her seat as she consulted her phone. 'About another hour and a half. We'll be there right in time for lunch!'

'Perfect.' Cooper's voice was bone-dry. 'A picnic with a polar bear. Just what I always dreamt of.'

'I knew you'd love it.' Dawn settled back into her seat with a satisfied grin.

Maybe this trip wouldn't be so unbearable after all.

Cooper stared up at the giant, glass-encased polar bear. He had to admit, he'd never seen bigger. Not that he'd actually been *looking*.

'Apparently, White King is ten feet four inches tall and weighs two thousand, two hundred pounds.' Dawn straightened up from reading the plaque beside the bear.

'I could have read that myself, you realise,' Cooper said.

Dawn gave a light shrug. 'It's more fun to learn these things together.'

Fun. Last he recalled, that wasn't what this road trip was about. Although, he had to admit, Dawn was a better travelling companion than he'd expected. She hadn't complained about the long hours in the car, or demanded to stop for bathroom breaks every thirty minutes. And she hadn't pressed too much to discover his secrets. It felt more as though she was using meaningless small talk—and polar bears—to distract herself from the end of the journey.

Which was interesting in itself.

'What I don't get is why this creature is *here*.' Cooper gestured around him at the casino and hotel that housed the giant bear, which seemed to have nothing to do with the Arctic Circle, as far as he could see.

Dawn peered down at her leaflet again. 'Apparently it was something to do with a competition to find the biggest polar bear, back in the fifties.'

Of course it was. Didn't everything come down to competition in the end? To proving you could be bigger or better or greater or richer than everyone else?

Cooper turned away from White King and sought out the bar menu instead. Cheap and cheerful was what they were going for, apparently.

'Hot dogs?' he suggested, and Dawn hesitated for a moment before nodding.

Then she grinned. 'It says here they'll bring your food to the slots, if you ask.'

Cooper frowned. 'So you're a gambler? Did my brother know?' Because that was exactly the sort of information that might have driven Justin away on his wedding day. A rich husband would certainly have solved the issue of any outstanding debts at the poker table…

But Dawn just laughed, as if he had to be joking. 'I've never actually been in a casino before. Not counting sleeping above one last night, of course. Justin and I talked about eloping to Vegas at one point, but…' She shook her head as she trailed off.

'But he wanted a proper family wedding, I assume.' Justin wouldn't have deprived their mother of the chance for a society event of the year, however stupidly in love he was.

'Actually, it was me.' Dawn flashed him a small smile. 'I knew my parents and my sisters would never forgive me if I just showed up married one day. And, besides, I'd waited long enough for a big day of my own.' She shrugged. 'Why skimp on it, right?'

'Especially when your fiancé has the money to give you your dream wedding,' Cooper replied. Of course she'd want the spectacle. What was the point of marrying into money if she couldn't show it off? Eloping would have defeated the object. If she was anything like Rachel—and, from Justin's note, he had to assume she was, even if she didn't always seem it—an elopement would have suggested a hasty mistake. She'd have wanted to show the world that she'd completely won Justin over, made him fall absurdly in love with her, before she dropped him and ran off, laughing all the way to the bank.

Dawn's smile stiffened. 'Yeah, well, weddings are always a compromise, aren't they? I mean, there's so many people to keep happy.'

Why would she care about that? That was the

part that Cooper couldn't figure out. Unless it was all part of the act, of course.

Rachel had designed every aspect of their wedding, and had kept control of the reins with an iron grip. The day hadn't been theirs, it had been hers, and everyone there had known it.

But, now that he thought about it, he hadn't seen much of the Dawn he'd come to know over the last three days in the arrangements for and Justin's and her wedding. And the guest list had been easily three-quarters full of people he knew his mother must have invited.

What he couldn't figure out was whether that meant she was less good at screwing his family over than Rachel, or more. Because, from speaking to his family after Justin's no-show, they'd seemed even more surprised—if not exactly disappointed—that the wedding hadn't gone ahead than Dawn had been.

'So, what do you think?' Dawn asked, her smile still a little too forced. 'Want to show me how to use these machines while we wait for our hot dogs? Perhaps White King here can be our lucky charm.'

Cooper stared across at the ringing, beeping,

irritating machines. It wasn't exactly *his* idea of a fun time, but at least it was something different from staring at the interstate for hours on end. Salt Lake City, where they'd decided to stop for the night, was still another three hours or more away, even if the traffic was good.

He rolled his eyes. 'Fine. Let's go get some change—as soon as I've ordered these hot dogs.'

Dawn's beaming smile was almost enough to make him forget why they were there in the first place, and the childish way she clapped her hands with glee was enough to make him doubt the only things he knew about her all over again.

She was a liar. She was after Justin's money.

So why was he having so much fun travelling with her?

CHAPTER SEVEN

'I'M PAYING FOR the hotel tonight,' Dawn reminded Cooper as the lights of Salt Lake City appeared on the horizon through the windscreen. Hopefully he'd take the hint and find somewhere affordable.

Cooper looked up from the hotel app on his phone. 'Planning on using your winnings from the historic commercial casino?'

'Ha! You'd better hope not, or we're sleeping on the streets tonight.' White King had, sadly, proved to be less of a lucky charm than she'd hoped.

'Yeah, I wouldn't turn to a career in professional gambling any time soon.' He scrolled through the pages of vacant hotel rooms on his phone, and Dawn tried to concentrate on the road rather than the prices on the screen. She'd have to check her card balance online when they stopped. Maybe she could up the credit limit...

'Okay, I've got us two rooms at a motel on the outskirts,' Cooper told her. 'Nothing fancy, but I figured we'd grab dinner first anyway, then just show up in time to sleep.'

Nothing fancy. In Cooper's world, that could mean anything, but at least it sounded as though he hadn't purposefully booked the most expensive place he could just to mess with her.

He had to know that she wasn't from the same sort of world as his brother and him—he'd met her family, after all. With five girls all at home, money had never exactly been abundant in the Featherington house—although, until she'd met Justin, Dawn had never felt badly off. Still, compared to the Edwards' world of beach houses in the Hamptons, vineyards in California and the ability to fly first class everywhere, Dawn supposed *most* people would feel kind of broke.

Of course, it was more her credit card bill that made her feel particularly poor these days. Because, while Justin had always been generous, he just hadn't always got that keeping up with the Edwards cost money. He'd happily pay for flights, holidays and dinners, but it wouldn't occur to him that the outfits he liked to show her off in, or the drink she needed to order at the fancy restaurant bar and sip slowly until he showed up an hour late for dinner, blaming work, were rather more expensive than she was used to paying for. Apparently Top Shop and a bottle of cider were *not* the Edwards' way.

She'd tried explaining it to Justin once or twice, but embarrassment meant she'd bungled it, hinting around the edges of the problem but never fully articulating it. Justin had just patted her hand and said how nice it was to date a girl with an actual job for a change, one who wasn't always looking for new ways to spend his money because she had her own.

But Dawn's job, good as it was, definitely hadn't paid for the same sort of lifestyle Justin was used to.

She just hoped Cooper was a bit more reasonable in his hotel expectations.

'Take a left off here,' Cooper said, glancing between the road and the map on his phone. 'There's a pancake house along here we can eat at, and the motel's not far after that.'

'Pancakes for dinner?' Dawn asked as she signalled. 'Aren't they more of a breakfast thing?'

Cooper shrugged. 'Why limit ourselves?'

'Fair point.'

The thing was, Dawn mused as she tucked into her chicken and mushroom cream sauce pancake a short while later, that until this week she'd always been more of a salads girl. At least, since she'd come over to the States. Firstly because her sisters had teased her about American portion sizes, and joked that she'd be as big as the other four of them put together by the time she came home again, and she'd really wanted to prove them wrong. And then, of course, having spent all that money on expensive clothes of the sort Justin liked, she really couldn't afford not to fit into them any more.

Besides, Justin liked her in bikinis, and they took a certain amount of self-discipline to look good in. Especially given the fact that most of the other women he introduced her to had nothing else to do with their time *but* make sure they looked good in bikinis. Dawn couldn't commit time or money to a personal trainer for three hours a day, plus nutritionally balanced meals delivered daily from a world-class chef, but she could order a plain salad when she ate out, and go for a run once in a while. So she had.

Until this week. Since Justin had failed to show up at the altar, she'd eaten a burger, doughnuts, hot dogs and now pancakes.

And she'd loved every delicious mouthful of them.

One thing was for certain—whatever happened with Justin, she was never going back to limiting herself to boring, tasteless food again.

They ate quickly, both tired and ready to get to the motel after a long day guiding Claudia across the country. Dawn drove the last mile or two to the motel, Cooper calling out directions from the satnav on his phone. As he guided her into the car park, Dawn let out a sigh of relief. The motel looked clean and respectable enough, but not as though it was going to break the bank. If they stuck to places like this, and she could get another five hundred dollars on her credit limit just in case, she should get away with paying for every other night's accommodation.

Of course, what she'd do after that was another worry entirely. One she'd deal with after she'd dealt with Justin.

'Let's go check in,' she said, breathing easily for the first time since they'd left White King behind. 'I've been dreaming of a bed to myself for the last hundred miles.'

Which, she decided later, was probably what had jinxed the whole thing.

'Yes, I am *absolutely* sure that I booked two rooms.' Cooper scraped a hand through his hair and glared at the teenager behind the motel desk who apparently had flunked maths every year since the first grade. 'Two. Not one. It's a fairly simple concept.'

'Yeah, but see, the thing is—' the boy started.

'The thing is *I need two rooms*!' Cooper roared, making the boy behind the desk jump. He'd feel guilty, except he was too exhausted to feel anything except tired. And maybe annoyed.

Dawn's hand on his arm caught his attention, and he turned to look at her.

'Let me?' she asked softly.

Cooper sighed and stepped back. 'By all means.'

'Hi!' Dawn beamed at the receptionist, looking perky and pleasant and nowhere near as tired as Cooper knew she had to be after driving all afternoon. 'So, my friend here booked us two rooms for tonight. Can we have them, please?'

'That's the thing! He didn't.' The boy leant over the desk, obviously relieved to be dealing with someone who would actually let him finish a sentence. Something that Cooper was fairly sure was a mistake, as the end of the sentence was usually, 'No,' in his experience.

'He absolutely did,' Dawn said. 'On your chain's booking app.'

The boy pulled a face. 'Oh, man, we've been having all sorts of problems with that thing. See, what he booked was one room for two adults.' He turned the computer screen so Dawn could see it, and Cooper watched her face fall. 'And that's the only room we have left.'

'Of course it is,' Dawn muttered, so low that Cooper had to strain to hear her. 'Because my life is apparently cursed.'

'So, uh, do you want the room?' The boy looked between the two of them, room key in his shaky hand.

This was ridiculous. Cooper reached across and plucked it from his hand. 'Which room?'

'Two-oh-two,' the boy replied, smiling with obvious relief.

Cooper grabbed his bag and motioned to Dawn. 'Come on.'

'So…we're sharing a room?' Dawn asked as they headed to room two hundred and two.

'Apparently so,' Cooper bit out.

'Right.' She did a quick double-step to catch him up, and Cooper realised he might be walking a little fast.

He was just so damned annoyed with himself. Or at least with the stupid booking app.

Spotting the number on a door, he halted suddenly, Dawn skidding a little beside him as she did the same.

Please let there be two beds. Please.

It was a long shot, he knew, given the quality of the motel, but Cooper had spent a long day in the car, and the few days before that hadn't been exactly relaxed, plus he'd hardly slept the night before. All he wanted to do was crawl into a soft bed and sleep for twelve solid hours. Was that so much to ask?

Apparently so.

The door swung open to reveal one bed that

could charitably be called a small double and an even smaller, lumpy-looking couch under the window.

Perfect.

Sighing, Cooper stepped in and flung his bag onto the floor by the couch. 'You take the bed,' he said, because he might be grumpy and exhausted but he was still a gentleman. 'I'll crash on the sofa.'

He was about to sit down on it and loosen his shoes when Dawn said, 'No.'

'No?' He looked up. Her expression was pure stubbornness, and he was just too tired for this.

'I'll take the sofa. I'm shorter—I'll fit better. You take the bed.' She folded her arms across her chest as if she was waiting for him to argue.

He *should* argue. That was the gentlemanly thing to do.

But he really wanted that bed…

No. 'Don't be silly. I'll take the couch.'

'I am not being silly.' Dawn's eyes grew harder, and he realised he might have chosen his words poorly. 'I'm being practical. The sofa is too short for you to sleep on, and it's your turn to drive first in the morning, so you need the rest more than me. I can sleep in the car tomorrow before I have to drive.'

When she put it like that, it did kind of make sense.

'Fine, if you insist.' Cooper gave her a tired smile. 'Thank you.'

Dawn nodded sharply. 'But I'm using the bathroom first,' she said, and flashed him a grin.

Maybe tonight wouldn't be too unbearable after all.

This was unbearable.

Dawn shifted between the lumps in the sofa's cushions, tugging the extra blanket they'd found in the wardrobe a little tighter around her. Just feet away, she could hear Cooper's slow, even breaths. At least one of them was getting some sleep. The bed, she thought rationally, probably wasn't all that comfortable either, given the general quality of the motel. But it had to be less awful than the sofa from hell.

Maybe she shouldn't have made such a fuss about giving him the bed. If she'd just let him play the gentleman, she could be curled up there asleep right now. Except then he'd have been grumpier than ever in the morning, and she didn't want to subject Claudia to his aggressive driving. Or herself to his glowering looks and sharp comments, come to that.

Sighing, Dawn turned over again, praying she'd find a comfortable position. She was being unfair to Cooper, she knew. So he wasn't thrilled to be spending his holiday on a road trip with a woman he barely knew. That was understandable. And actually, over the last day or so, he'd started to lighten up. They'd even had a beer each with their pancakes when they'd stopped and, although they'd been too tired to talk much, there had at least been a weary comradeship building between them, she thought.

Until the whole room debacle, anyway.

There was, she realised now, a third option for sleeping arrangements—one that neither of them even seemed to have considered. It had only occurred to Dawn once she was settled on the sofa with a spring stuck in her back.

They could have shared the bed.

For one brief, blissful moment, Dawn let herself consider how it might feel to lie on an actual mattress, with enough space to stretch her legs out the whole way. With a real duvet, instead of this scratchy, itchy wool blanket. With Cooper's arms wrapped warm around her and…

Wait. No.

Where the hell had that come from?

A place of sleep deprivation, Dawn decided, as she turned her back on the bed and stared, wide-eyed, at the cushions of the sofa.

She was not thinking about Justin's brother that way. And, actually, she really wasn't. What she was imagining was warmth, comfort and another person beside her who wasn't just there because…

Why *was* Cooper there, anyway? What was it about her that made him want to drive cross-country just to be there with her when she saw Justin again? She was under no illusion that Cooper was doing this to get them back together again, so he must be planning to make sure that Dawn didn't try to win Justin back.

But why? What was it he disliked so much about her?

She sighed. Another mystery to add to the list of things she didn't understand about Cooper

Dawn to be someone else. Someone with high expectations, and doing a lot of whining when he didn't meet them. He'd expected her to be annoyed at the long hours in the car and never offer to drive, horrified by the tacky motels he kept choosing for them to stay in and disgusted by the idea of hot dogs for lunch and pancakes for dinner. He'd expected Dawn to fleece him for nights in five-star hotels and insist on dressing up for dinner in the fanciest restaurants.

He'd expected Dawn to be just like his ex-wife, Rachel.

Instead, he'd got the woman who wanted to stop off to see giant polar bears, and drove the Caddy with the sort of love and affection he showed her himself. And had actually *named* her, come to that.

He hadn't been mentally prepared for Dawn. That much was clear.

That was one of the reasons he'd set his alarm so early. Because, when they'd settled into their room together the night before, just for a moment he'd imagined them heading out and grabbing breakfast together the next morning. He'd thought of suggesting they take in Gilgal Gardens before they hit the road, because if she thought the giant polar bear was quirky she really hadn't seen anything yet. He'd even considered, just for a moment, suggesting they share the damn bed.

But then he'd remembered his brother's note, remembered who she really was, interest in kitsch roadside attractions aside. So when he'd opened his mouth to say goodnight, he'd found himself saying, 'I want to hit the road by seven. We can stop for coffee and breakfast on the way. It's ten and a half hours to Lexington, and we can make it in a day if we don't hang around.'

That was what mattered. Getting to Justin quickly and ending this.

Then he'd turned over in the bed, his back to her couch, already regretting the overreaction that meant spending over ten hours stuck in Claudia's overheating seats the following day.

He regretted it even more now, as the alarm went off again, and he levered himself out of bed to wait for his turn in the shower. But then he remembered what roadside surprises Interstate 80 had for them today and he couldn't help but smile.

Maybe this road trip had started out as an obligation. But did that really have to mean it couldn't be fun too?

CHAPTER EIGHT

BY THE TIME Cooper was done with his shower, and had packed up his few belongings, Dawn was already waiting for him in the lobby, paying the motel bill for the night before. Cooper faltered slightly as he approached when he realised what she was doing. Yes, she'd said she would, but he hadn't actually believed it.

The woman made no sense. The only possible explanation that fitted with Justin's letter was that she was trying to prove him wrong—trying to show Cooper that the money wasn't important to her, so that he didn't interfere with her plans to win Justin back.

The only problem with that theory was that Cooper had been with women like that before—women who liked to live the high life on credit to enable them to move in the circles that meant they could find a rich husband to pay it off. And Dawn, with her hair scraped back in a high ponytail, wearing the same denim skirt as yesterday with another cheap and colourful tee shirt, did not fit that mould.

His instincts told him that Dawn wasn't trying to be anything right now. She was just being herself. And that made no sense at all. So either his instincts were wrong or there was something else going on here that he didn't understand.

Who the hell was this woman Justin had run out on? And why did it bother Cooper so much that he couldn't read her the way he read every other woman he met these days?

'Ready to go?' Dawn asked, smiling cautiously at him, probably in response to the frown he could feel creasing his forehead.

'Yep. Let's go see how Claudia fared for the night, shall we?' He tried to make his words friendly, and saw Dawn's shoulders relax a little for the effort.

Claudia was as steady and reliable as ever, and Cooper slipped behind the steering wheel with relief. This, at least, he understood. The classic car, the open road, travelling to reach a destination—that all made sense.

The woman in the seat beside him, less so.

He swung into a drive-through to pick up coffee and breakfast muffins before they left the city, then headed back out on the interstate. Dawn seemed quieter this morning—maybe more tired than ever after her night on the couch. She dozed for a bit, but even after she woke up she didn't seem to have much to say.

After about an hour, the silence grew a little too oppressive as they drove through the hills out of Utah into Wyoming. Cooper switched on the radio, hoping for something not terrible, and grinned when Elvis crackled through the speakers.

'Seems appropriate,' Dawn said, returning his smile. 'Claudia, the open road and Elvis. I'm basically living the American cliché right here.'

'If it were the nineteen-fifties, maybe,' Cooper admitted. 'This is more of a nostalgia trip than reality, I think.'

'You're probably right. Still, it's nice to imagine.' She sounded strangely wistful as Elvis sang of lost love and heartache.

'So, is this what you were imagining when you moved Stateside?' Cooper asked, curiosity getting the better of him. 'Being an all-American housewife, baking apple pies and driving places with the hood down?'

Dawn laughed. 'Do you think I'd have agreed to marry Justin if it was? That's not exactly the sort of lives you guys live, is it?'

'No, I suppose not.' With the Edwards brothers, it had always been work hard and play harder. Until Rachel, of course. Then, for Cooper at least, it had become 'work hard and forget'.

'But… I guess… I grew up on stories from my mum—she's American, did you know?' Dawn said, and Cooper nodded to show he remembered. 'She grew up here in the sixties, and apparently her mother was very much that all-American housewife you talk about. Her family were quintessential middle America, I guess. All the clichés you can imagine.'

'So what took her to England?'

'My dad. They met when he was over here on a road trip of his own, actually. They fell in love fast, and her parents thought she was crazy when she said yes to his proposal after only two weeks.'

'Hardly surprising,' Cooper pointed out. He'd proposed to Rachel after only a month—and look what an almighty screw-up that had turned out to be.

'But she stood her ground. They got married less than a month later and moved to England together.' She paused and Cooper waited, knowing that couldn't be the end of that story. 'My wedding-that-wasn't was the first time she'd been back in almost forty years.'

Cooper's eyebrows shot up. 'Wow. Talk about burning bridges, huh?'

Dawn gave a small, embarrassed-looking shrug. 'I guess my grandparents *really* didn't approve of the marriage. But, the thing is, she talked about her life here, growing up, so often that it felt real to me. And so when I got the opportunity to come and work over here it felt like a no-brainer, you know?'

'Did you track down any of your family?'

'No,' Dawn said, turning to look out of the window. 'My grandparents both died years ago, and Mum was an only child. So there didn't seem much point, really. I wanted to come here for me, to see what it was really like. And then I met Justin.'

'And fell madly in love.' Cooper didn't try very

hard to keep the sarcasm out of his voice, but Dawn didn't even seem to notice.

'Yeah. I did.' She smiled down at her hands shyly, as if embarrassed by it. 'The funny thing is, everything happened so fast it was almost scary. And Justin... His world wasn't mine, and sometimes I felt so out of my depth. But then I realised it couldn't be half as terrifying as what my mum had been through for love. So I just let myself go with it. Of course, with hindsight...' Her smile turned rueful.

'Would you do things the same?' Cooper asked. 'If you'd known how things would turn out?'

Dawn bit down on her lip before answering, obviously giving the question far more thought than Cooper thought it deserved.

'Yes,' she said eventually. 'I think I would.'

Would she have done things the same? Would she have risked getting stood up by Justin on her wedding day all over again, and then taken off cross-country with his brother on a crazy road trip?

Who in their right mind would bring all that on themselves *twice*?

Well, she would, it seemed. Because, try as she might, Dawn couldn't imagine living her life in a way that didn't take that sort of chance to find a 'for ever' love. Couldn't imagine *not* jumping at the chance for happiness.

Was that how her mother had felt all those years ago? Suddenly, Cooper's question made her feel closer to her mum than she had in years.

'It's funny,' she said, smiling. 'All these years, I've thought I was nothing like the rest of my family—especially my mum and my sisters. But maybe I have more in common with them than I think.'

'You all fall in love too fast?' Cooper asked, and she knew he was being sarcastic, but he was also *right,* so she nodded.

'We all take a chance on love,' she amended. 'Some of us more often than others.'

'Ah, so you've done this a lot, then?' Cooper's tone wasn't surprised—more as if she was confirming something about herself that he'd long suspected. Although why he'd been thinking about her past romantic entanglements Dawn couldn't imagine.

'Not *lots,* exactly.' Dawn winced as she wondered what the exact definition of 'lots' was, anyway. 'Let's just say I haven't always been particularly lucky in love.'

'I noticed,' Cooper said drily.

Shifting in her seat, Dawn looked past him out of the windscreen rather than continue the conversation. Then she frowned.

'What is *that*?'

Cooper didn't even look before he answered. Apparently he'd known this was coming.

'It's the giant head of Abraham Lincoln.' There, on the side of the road, a huge statue stood over them, judging them.

'That's…kind of what I was afraid you were going to say.' Dawn stared out at the looming figure high over the interstate, staring down at the traffic. 'Um, why is it there?'

Cooper shrugged. 'Hard to say. I think it used to loom over the Lincoln Highway, which at least made some sense. Then it got moved, well, here.'

'Because that is a totally normal thing to do,'

Dawn said, staring out of the window as Cooper drove past the giant bronze head.

Huh. America.

Maybe her mum had been right to get out while she had the chance.

'This is the country of extremes,' Cooper pointed out. 'Extreme wealth, extreme poverty, extreme temperatures…'

'And extreme statues,' Dawn finished for him. 'I get it.'

'Just wait until you see what's coming up next.' Cooper smirked at her, then turned his gaze back to the road.

Dawn didn't have to wait long. About fifteen minutes by Claudia's clock—although she had no idea how accurate that was.

'Okay, that's less bizarre than the giant head,' she admitted. 'But what *is* it?'

'It's a tree. Don't you have those in Britain?'

'Not growing out of solid rock in the middle of the road we don't.' At least, not that she'd ever seen.

They were in the middle of Wyoming, with bright blue skies and scorched brown earth all around them, the interstate a river of grey in the landscape. And there, right in the centre of I-80, stood a tree. Lopsided and windswept, and maybe a little stunted, but a living tree. Growing right out of a piece of what looked like granite.

'That takes some perseverance,' Dawn said as they sailed past the plucky little tree. 'I mean, the road even goes *around* it.'

'Story goes that when they were building the first railroad along this route the railroad men were so impressed with that stubborn little limber pine, they actually moved the railroad so as not to disturb it.' Even Cooper sounded vaguely impressed by the tree's pluckiness. 'Then, by the time the railroad moved and they wanted to put the interstate in, the tree was too famous to shift, so they made the road go around it.'

'Huh.' The tree in the road zoomed out of sight, and Dawn turned back in her seat, settling down again, thinking hard.

'Huh?' Cooper repeated. 'It's just a tree, Dawn.'

'No, it isn't.' She hadn't even got a decent look at the thing, but she already knew it was more than that. It was a parable. A promise. 'It's hope.'

'Hope?' Cooper's tone was even more derisory

than normal, which Dawn hadn't been entirely sure was possible.

'Yeah. Hope.' The more she said it, the more sure she was. 'Think how many other seeds must have tried to grow into trees in that place and failed. All the saplings that didn't survive their first winter. Or seeds that landed on stone and just rotted. But not that one.'

'I guess.'

'That seed flourished, even though it shouldn't,' Dawn went on, warming to her theme. 'That tree grew in the most unlikely place, defying all the odds. And it was that defiance that kept it alive when the railways or the roads should have destroyed it. It was the hope it gave people—the promise of survival against impossible odds. It's basically American history in horticulture.'

Cooper laughed. 'Maybe you're right.'

'Of course I'm right.' And, if a tree could do it, why couldn't she? That little pine hadn't given up, so why should Dawn? 'Haven't you ever succeeded at something against all the odds, against all the people who told you that you couldn't?'

It was the wrong question, clearly. Cooper's face closed down instantly. 'Mostly I like to stack the odds in my favour first, to assure success. It's just good business.'

'Yeah, but there must have been something you stuck at, or went ahead with, even when it seemed hopeless?' She could tell there had been. If there hadn't been, Cooper wouldn't have reacted that way.

'Nothing that ended well,' he said darkly, and Dawn winced.

'Well, *I'm* going to be more like that tree,' she said firmly. Then she risked a cheeky smile in his direction. 'You can be more like the giant bronze head of Abraham Lincoln, if you like.'

He didn't dignify that with a response, and Dawn only just held in her laughter.

Cooper wasn't sure why he insisted on driving so far that day when they were both already so tired, but he suspected it had something to do with Dawn's musings on succeeding against the odds and perseverance.

The only time he'd ever done anything that smacked of defying conventional wisdom was when he'd fallen in love with Rachel. Hell, it hadn't been even just conventional wisdom he'd defied—it had been his own. He'd known better, and he'd fallen anyway.

He hadn't been in love with Melanie, back when he'd been twenty-one and his mother had asked him to show her around the company and teach her the ropes—but he knew he could have fallen, if she'd let him. She'd been a student on a summer placement, and he'd been showing off because she was beautiful and he wanted to impress her. She'd flirted, smiled and let him think that he mattered, that he was important. He'd been so full of himself he'd let all sorts of company secrets slip—and she'd turned around and given them to her boyfriend, who'd just happened to work for their biggest competitor.

Coming back from that, proving to his father and the board that he could be trusted again, had been one of the hardest things he'd ever had to do. But he'd done it by setting his own rules. By understanding that everyone wanted something from you, and you had to figure out the cost before you decided if it was worth paying.

Then his dad had died and he'd taken over the company, and for a long time work had been more important than anything else. And, when he'd finally had time to breathe again, he'd known who he was. He'd known what he had—money and power. He'd known what people wanted from him. And he'd made damn sure only to give it away on his own terms—until Rachel.

Rachel had broken past his walls, made him believe that she wanted something else, something no one had ever wanted from him before. Love.

He'd given it all to her—and it had nearly destroyed him.

Love, he'd decided, was the most illogical thing of all.

But he had a feeling that the damned tree in the rock had inspired Dawn to go and chase it again.

Just hopefully not with his brother.

They swapped seats after a swift late lunch in a roadside diner, Dawn sliding in behind Claudia's wheel as if she'd been driving her all her life. She cranked up the radio—still playing Elvis—and started singing along, mangling the words so badly that Cooper couldn't help but join in on the chorus.

She beamed at him as he sang, and he rolled his eyes and pretended he wasn't really singing, even though he obviously was.

Still, as the skies started to grow orange and red as the daylight faded, Dawn looked exhausted.

'Are we planning to stop soon?' she asked, the question truncated by a jaw-cracking yawn.

'Lexington,' he said shortly. 'About another hour.'

'Right.' Another yawn, and Claudia swerved slightly as Dawn took her hand off the wheel to cover her mouth again.

Cooper swore silently. She wasn't going to make it to Lexington. She'd hardly slept the night before, because she'd given him the bed. And, as much as his aching arms didn't want to drive any more today either, he would have to take over the wheel or risk them crashing.

Maybe Lexington *was* too far to aim for tonight. But he knew they had to make it, all the same. He had to get to Justin, to help his brother escape making the same mistake he had.

He glanced across at Dawn again, her eyes sleepy but her jaw set. He couldn't help but think she'd be a better match for any man than Rachel had been, but what did he know? His swift divorce was proof that he was no judge of women.

Maybe Dawn was just a better actress than his ex-wife.

Up ahead, Cooper saw lights and a familiar sign, and smiled.

'Pull over at the next turn-off,' he said. 'We'll swap over.'

Dawn frowned as she signalled. 'Here?'

'Yep,' Cooper replied as the giant likeness of Buffalo Bill came into view. 'Right here.'

It had been *years* since Cooper had been to Fort Cody, the replica frontier-redoubt that claimed to be Nebraska's largest souvenir and Western gift store. He struggled even to remember how they'd come across it, or why they'd even been travelling through Nebraska in the first place— it certainly wasn't the sort of place the Edwards family had frequented when he'd been growing up. But that was precisely why Cooper liked it so much.

'Fort Cody Trading Post,' Dawn read doubtfully. 'Western gifts?'

'It's a souvenir place, mostly.' Cooper unbuckled his seat belt. 'With a bit of frontier history thrown in. Come on.'

Dawn's uncertain expression started to fade as she took in the log stockade walls and the wooden lookout towers with the stars and stripes flying from them.

'So is this where the real Buffalo Bill came from?' she asked, reading the information board under the giant, thirty-foot-tall Bill Cody sign.

'Well, maybe not originally,' Cooper allowed. 'But he lived here for a while.'

'I suppose that counts.' Dawn flashed him a cheeky grin. 'I suppose when a country only has a few centuries of history you have to take what you can get.'

'Of course, even when a country is as vast and influential as the United States, it's still quite an achievement to have so much history everywhere you travel within it,' Cooper countered, and Dawn laughed.

'I'll let you have that one,' she said, linking her hand through his arm casually. He stiffened at her touch, then forced himself to relax. 'Come on, let's go in. I have a lot of family to buy souvenirs for.'

She didn't let go until they were well inside, when she dashed off to study some Buffalo Bill keyrings, and suddenly Cooper felt a chill, despite the warmth of the evening.

Unsettled, he watched Dawn flit from stand to stand within the main shop, collecting tacky memorabilia in her arms as though it was precious jewels, holding it close against her chest. She looked like a child in a sweet shop, and Cooper tried to remember the last time he'd seen such sheer enjoyment in anyone.

He couldn't. But, if he could, he knew for a fact it wouldn't have been caused by a Buffalo Bill keyring.

The people in his life—work colleagues, family, a few acquaintances that had hung around after his divorce—weren't the sort of people to get excited by souvenirs and *faux* Western decoration. None of them. If he'd brought literally anyone else he knew to this place, they'd have rolled their eyes at the spectacle and told him they'd wait in the car.

Which led him to the very uncomfortable

conclusion that Dawn wasn't like anyone else he knew.

Maybe that wasn't too bad in itself, but it was the thought it led to next that was causing him real problems.

'I just need to go pay for these, then we'll get some coffee, okay?' Dawn said, bouncing up next to him, her arms full.

Cooper just nodded and watched her bound away again towards the shop desk.

If Dawn wasn't like anyone he knew, she wasn't like Rachel. And spending the last few days in her company had led him to only one disturbing conclusion. One he knew in his gut was absolutely true, even if it made no sense at all.

Justin was wrong about her.

So what the hell did he do now?

CHAPTER NINE

THEY RAN INTO a traffic jam not far outside Lexington, stuck in a long line of stationary cars just a few miles from the hotel Cooper had booked while they'd been at Fort Cody, while the sky grew darker and night time fell. Dawn was relieved that Cooper was driving, not sure that she'd have been able to stay alert enough to deal with the stop-start traffic and the idiots trying to pull unsafe manoeuvres to get them home sooner.

But, as Cooper's jaw cracked with a huge yawn, she realised that she wasn't the only one who was tired, and it was her duty as a road-trip buddy to keep him awake and attentive.

Which meant it was time for the time-honoured tradition of car games. Starting with Fortunately/Unfortunately.

'Fortunately, we're not too far from our hotel,' she said with a perky smile.

Cooper narrowed his eyes at her. 'Unfortunately it could take us hours through all this traffic.'

'Fortunately, we're in the best car in the world!'

'What are we doing here?' Cooper asked, and Dawn clicked her tongue with disappointment.

'That's not the game!'

'We're playing a game?'

Dawn shook her head. 'Don't you know anything? We're on a road trip, we're stuck in traffic. We have to play games.'

'Do I at least get to know the rules, then?' Cooper looked faintly amused at the prospect of car games, which Dawn decided was probably the best reaction she could expect from him.

'It's easy. I say something positive and optimistic—like, fortunately we're not far from our hotel—and you do what apparently comes totally naturally to you, since you didn't even realise we were playing, and say something negative, like—'

'Unfortunately it could take hours,' Cooper finished for her.

'Exactly!' She grinned at him. 'Ready now?'

'Hang on. Why can't I do the "fortunately" part?' Cooper asked.

Dawn blinked. 'Uh, I guess you could. If you liked.' And if he honestly thought he could come up with positive things to say for the next twenty minutes, or for however long they would be stuck in this traffic jam. 'I suppose it could be more of a challenge that way round.'

Because *she* was the positive one. The one always looking for a happy-ever-after. And he… well, wasn't.

'Fortunately, I like a challenge,' Cooper said. And just like that, the game was on.

'Unfortunately for you, I am a champion at this game.'

'Fortunately for me, I'm a quick learner,' Cooper countered.

'Unfortunately, you're an eternal pessimist.' Okay, that was a little harsh, but Dawn was playing to win.

'Fortunately, I've been taking lessons in optimism from you.'

'Unfortunately, my optimism is at an all-time low—after being, you know, jilted on my wedding day—so I might not be such a great teacher.'

Cooper gave her a soft smile. 'Fortunately, I know it would take more than that to keep you down.'

Dawn felt a strange warmth filling her at his words. Was he right? She hoped so. 'Um... Unfortunately... Damn.' She couldn't think of anything.

'Want to switch to I Spy?' Cooper asked, and Dawn nodded. Much safer.

An hour or so later, Dawn sank down onto the hotel room bed, closed her eyes and smiled. Cooper had insisted on finding somewhere a little nicer to stay in Lexington, after the disaster at the motel the night before—adding that he'd cover it before she even had time to worry about the hit to her credit card—and she really hadn't been able to say no. The fluffy bathrobe, power shower and ridiculously comfortable mattress almost made her forget that she'd spent most of the last two days in a car. And possibly a significant portion of her remaining money on Buffalo Bill keyrings for her family.

'Are you sure you've got enough of those?' Cooper had asked, nodding at her heavy bag as she'd carried it in from the car after an epic game of I Spy.

She'd shrugged. 'I have a lot of family who flew a long way for a wedding that didn't happen. I figure the least I owe them is a keyring. I kind of wanted to get the moose's head for Dad, but that would be a nightmare to ship, so…keyrings all round.'

Cooper, she'd noticed, hadn't bought anything at all, despite how excited he'd looked at stopping there. She wondered if it had been some sort of childhood favourite, one that Justin had shared, although Justin had never mentioned it.

She'd half-thought that Cooper might have bought something for his brother, but he hadn't. She hadn't either, after some consideration. Showing up with gifts would smack a little too much of her coming after him to grovel, to beg him to come back. And the more distance she got from the wedding the more certain she was that she didn't want to do that.

And only a little bit of that reasoning was down to Cooper.

Dawn couldn't get a good read on him. One minute he was laughing and calling their car

Claudia, stopping for ridiculously huge boxes of doughnuts for the journey, pulling over at stupidly fun roadside attractions or playing road-trip games. That Cooper she liked, could relax with and even enjoy his company.

It was the other Cooper who was causing her problems. The one who glared at her when she cracked a joke, who shifted the conversation away from any question she asked about his past or his personal life. The one who looked at her so hard sometimes she felt as though he were trying to see right through her skin, right to the heart of her.

She wondered what he saw there. She hadn't quite found the courage to ask yet.

A knock on the door pulled her from her reverie, and she groaned as she forced herself to her feet to answer it. Probably room service with the wrong room. Even nice hotels seemed to screw that up sometimes.

'I didn't order anything— Oh. Hi.'

Cooper stood outside her door, dark eyes warm in the dim lights of the hotel corridor. 'You left this in Claudia.' He held out her phone charger; it must have fallen out of her bag, she realised.

She really needed to buy a proper bag to keep her stuff in, rather than relying on a ratty carrier bag. 'I figured you'd probably need it tonight.'

'I hadn't even noticed it was missing,' Dawn said, reaching out to take it from him. 'Thanks.'

He shrugged nonchalantly. 'No bother.'

'What were you doing back at the car anyway?' she asked.

Cooper's expression turned furtive. 'Nothing. Just…checking something.'

Had he been planning to leave? To abandon her here in the middle of nowhere, Nebraska? And, if so, what made him change his mind?

Her suspicions must have shown on her face, because Cooper sighed. 'Look, I wasn't making a run for it, I promise. I just needed to clear my head, so I went for a walk and found myself at the car. Your charger was sitting on the front seat. I didn't drive a yard.'

'You were sitting in the car imagining you were some fifties movie star, weren't you?' Dawn joked, mostly to distract herself from the overwhelming relief flooding through her. He *hadn't* been leaving her.

'Something like that.' Cooper gave her a small, lopsided smile. 'I guess I find Claudia calming.'

'You are the only person I know who, after spending basically a whole day sitting in a car, would voluntarily head back out there to sit in it some more even though you weren't getting anywhere.'

'Who said I wasn't getting anywhere?' Cooper asked.

Dawn frowned. 'You said you didn't drive anywhere.'

'No, but that's not always the same thing.' Leaning against the doorframe, Cooper looked at her—that deep-down, searching look she could never read properly—and Dawn tried not to flinch under his gaze. 'I had some thinking to do, was all.'

'About life, the universe and everything?' Dawn asked flippantly.

'About you.' By contrast, Cooper's tone was a hundred per cent serious.

'Me?' Dawn wasn't sure she liked the thought of that. What was there to think about, anyway? She liked to think she was a pretty open book.

'Yeah. You're a puzzle, Dawn Featherington.'

'I'm really not.' Somehow, as they talked, she'd leaned in closer to him, so she was half-way through the doorway herself. She just hoped no other guests happened on them. Their conversation must look far more intimate than it really was. Yet Dawn couldn't quite bring herself to pull away. 'What are you trying to figure out? Just ask me and I'll tell you.'

She would, Dawn realised. She'd answer any question he had, just to get him to stop looking at her as if he was seeking out all her secrets.

Or maybe to make sure he never stopped.

She wasn't entirely sure.

And *that,* right there, was a problem.

Dawn stepped back away from the doorframe, away from Cooper and his too-knowing eyes. He was her almost-brother-in-law, nothing else. The last thing she needed was to be sharing secrets and *moments* with this man.

Cooper looked as if he understood, because his smile turned sad. 'Ah, but where would be the fun in that?' he asked, and it took her a full minute to remember what she'd offered.

He pushed away from the doorframe and

raised a hand in farewell. 'I'll see you in the morning, Dawn.'

'Eight in the lobby?' she guessed.

Cooper was already halfway down the hallway towards his own room a few doors down but he threw his answer back over his shoulder. 'Let's make it nine. We can get pancakes before we leave.'

It wasn't until she saw him disappear into his own room that Dawn shut the door, leaning against it and breathing deeply.

They'd talked about practically nothing. He'd returned her phone charger. They'd made plans for the morning, just like the last couple of nights.

So why did she feel suddenly as if everything had changed?

Cooper was already regretting the previous night's indulgence with the minibar by the time Dawn met him in the lobby. He'd known, after their conversation in her doorway, that he should just get some sleep. If sitting in Claudia examining his every interaction with Dawn so far hadn't given him a better understanding of whatever game she was playing—or the possibility that Justin had been mistaken—he definitely wasn't going to find any answers at the bottom of a miniature bottle of alcohol. Or even several miniature bottles.

But he'd tried anyway. And, by the time he'd dragged himself to bed and to sleep, he'd been drunk and clueless instead of just clueless. Perfect.

'Pancakes?' Dawn asked in greeting, her tone far too annoyingly cheerful for nine in the morning.

'We should get going,' he replied shortly, then cursed inwardly as her face fell. 'But there's probably time for pancakes,' he conceded, cursing himself even more.

What was it about this woman?

The problem, he'd decided last night, a couple of bottles in, was that he was starting from a place of incomplete information. Gut instinct aside, all he really knew was: A: Justin loved Dawn, but also believed her to be a gold-digger, and B: Dawn was willing to drive all the way across the country with him to win Justin back. Even if she denied it, it was pretty obvious to him.

Those two pieces of information alone should have been enough to compel him to keep his interactions with Dawn to a minimum, or at least keep his distance emotionally. He didn't need to know her secrets, didn't need to understand her motivations.

But apparently knowing that wasn't enough to make him stop trying.

Worst of all was the realisation that had driven him to drink the night before: as he'd stood in her hotel doorway, taking in her fluffy bathrobe and handing her the stupid phone charger she'd left behind *again*, he'd realised he wanted to kiss her.

And that was, put simply, the worst idea anyone had ever had. Ever.

He reminded himself of that several times over breakfast: every time she tried to start a conversation with him that hit too close to the personal, when she smiled and thanked their waiter so graciously, and especially when she licked syrup off her lip with more enthusiasm than Cooper felt was really necessary.

Although, they were damned good pancakes. Even his bad mood couldn't hide that.

They'd been on the road for almost two hours before Dawn tried talking to him again; apparently his grumpiness at breakfast had warned her off, as he'd intended. But a couple of hours of open road and Claudia purring through the landscape had improved his mindset, as he reminded himself he just had to take what he could from this experience and focus on helping his brother at the end of it. Everything else could go hang.

'You know, the world's biggest time capsule isn't far from here, in Seward,' Dawn said, her tone tentative. 'I mean, if you fancied swapping drivers anyway…'

'You want to stop and see it?' Cooper asked. Time capsules weren't really his thing. Although the idea of locking up the past and forgetting about it appealed, the thought that he'd have to dig it up and re-examine it again one day was less enjoyable.

'Well, I just thought…it could be interesting, that's all.'

Cooper didn't answer. But, when he saw the turn-off for Seward, he took it, all the same.

Dawn tilted her head as she stared at the large, white concrete pyramid set in the garden of a house in suburban Seward, Nebraska.

'The plaque says the original time capsule was buried in 1975, then the pyramid was added on top eight years later.' Cooper peered closer at the bronze plaque. 'Apparently there's even a couple of *cars* in there, for some reason.'

His tone held the same disinterest it had all morning, and Dawn wondered for the hundredth time what it was she'd done to force that distance between them. She told herself she only wanted to know so she could make sure to keep doing it—the last thing she needed was to give in to any fleeting attraction to Justin's brother.

But the truth was she wanted the camaraderie back. The way they'd been the second day or so of their trip, when everything had been new and exciting and she'd been focused on her goal.

Before she'd started staring at Cooper's lips when he talked.

Before she'd ever imagined what it might feel like to kiss him.

Did he know? Was that why he was pulling away?

Or did he really, truly have something against time capsules, since her suggestion to visit this one seemed to be what had set off this particular round of his hiding-behind-his-shades, don't-touch-me vibe.

Dawn really hoped it was the time capsule. Otherwise, it was going to be a very long few days to the Hamptons and Justin.

'What would you put in your capsule?' she asked, hoping to draw out any childhood traumas with time capsules that might be affecting him.

Cooper just shrugged. 'I don't know. What are you supposed to put in these things?'

'Items that represent your life right now, I suppose.' Dawn glanced at the plaque, hoping for guidance, but it was no help. It just told her that the thing wasn't to be opened until 2025.

Where would she be by then? Dawn had no idea, but it almost certainly wouldn't be Seward, Nebraska.

'Then probably the work file for the latest deal I'm working on,' Cooper said with a shrug.

Dawn turned away from the pyramid to stare at him instead. 'Seriously? That's the only thing you can think of? Nothing personal at all?'

Did he really have *no* personal life? She knew from Justin's few comments that Cooper was the ultimate workaholic, but surely even the most dedicated CEO had to have *some* friendships, hobbies or interests outside of the office?

'A pair of running shoes?' Cooper tried. Because *of course* he stayed in shape. Even she'd noticed that. Okay, so she'd noticed that quite a lot, since his new wardrobe of thin cotton tee shirts and jeans did rather more to show off his body than the suit and tuxedo she'd seen him in before.

'Let me guess, exercise is important because it helps you work longer hours, right?'

'And live longer,' Cooper added. 'Thus staving off retirement by a few more years.'

'Of course.' Dawn sighed. The man really *was* hopeless. 'So, no friendships or relationships you want to commemorate?'

Cooper's expression turned contemplative. 'I

suppose I *could* throw in my wedding ring and a copy of my divorce decree, but I don't think that's the sort of upbeat, inspiring content you're looking for here.'

'I don't suppose it is,' Dawn said quietly. What had happened to make this man so bitter about people—especially love? He'd be amiable enough when they chatted about nothing in the car, or in the various diners they stopped in en route, but the moment she got close to anything personal he'd clam up. He liked to pretend that he cared for nothing and nobody outside the office, but here he was escorting her across the country to find his brother and her closure.

She didn't understand him.

But she really, really wanted to—even if she wasn't ready to admit why, yet, even to herself.

'What happened with your wife?' This was the closest Cooper had really got to talking about her since they'd met, and Dawn wasn't going to miss the chance to find out more—to obtain another piece of the complicated puzzle that was Cooper Edwards.

'Actually, it was rather like your parents' story. And yours and Justin's, to a point,' he said. 'Whirlwind romance, sudden wedding—except in my case it featured an even more sudden divorce.'

'At least you got to the actually married stage,' Dawn joked. Cooper didn't laugh.

She swallowed uncomfortably before asking, 'Where is she now?'

'Last I heard, she'd moved to Seattle with a wealthy cosmetic surgeon and was planning another wedding.' Cooper didn't look at her as he spoke, and his words were completely devoid of emotion. Dawn felt sympathy welling up inside her.

'You must have loved her very much,' she said, trying to imagine Cooper ever feeling enough for anyone to propose—let alone falling desperately in love in just a few weeks. She couldn't.

'Rather more than she ever loved me, as it turned out.' He flashed her a bitter smile. 'I don't suppose that's quite what *you* were expecting from marriage.'

'Well, for starters I was expecting my groom to show up,' Dawn pointed out. 'But beyond that, yeah, I guess I was expecting true love. The "for ever" kind. Like my parents have.'

'I'm not sure mine ever did,' Cooper admitted. 'Even before Dad died, things were tense between them. And Mom…she knew what she married into with the Edwards family and she's always played the role perfectly. I guess I believed Rachel would do the same.'

'But she wasn't interested?' Dawn guessed.

Cooper's smile fell away. 'Not exactly. But enough about her. What about you? Would you be truly happy playing at being Mrs Edwards, matriarch and upholder of Edwards family values once Mom is gone?'

The question sounded too pointed to be just a casual one, and Dawn resisted her natural urge just to laugh at it. For some reason, this mattered to Cooper. He really wanted to know her answer. So the least she could do was consider it properly.

'I don't know,' she said slowly, surprised by her own admission. If anyone had asked her the night before her wedding, she was sure she'd have said yes in a heartbeat. As it was… 'I guess I never really imagined that far ahead. I just thought about me and Justin being together, blissfully happy. Perhaps with a family—a couple of kids, a boy and a girl. I thought about summers together at the beach house, and Christmas together, one year in Britain the next over here. I thought about quiet moments, just the two of us. But I didn't think so much about the Edwards legacy or any of that.' She gave him a rueful smile. 'Maybe, in my mind, I sort of assumed that you'd get married again and your wife would take care of all that.'

'Well, that's never going to happen. So maybe it's for the best that Justin didn't show up at the altar.' Leaving her speechless, Cooper walked back towards Claudia, whose robin's-egg-blue paintwork was shining in the midday sun. Apparently the conversation was over.

Was that truly what bothered him about her—that she wasn't suitable enough to take on the Edwards legacy? That she wouldn't be able to step into his mother's shoes in the future?

Maybe he was right about that. But Dawn couldn't help but feel that there was something more to the story that she was missing.

Either way, his comments had cut deeper than she'd like, and she made a point of staying away from Claudia for longer than she otherwise would have, until she'd recovered her equilibrium. She tried to take in the details about the time capsule—the controversy about whether the large space underground that formed most of it really *was* the biggest in the world, which had resulted in the additional pyramid on top, and the fact that Guinness had actually dropped the category from their world records shortly after, so it didn't really even count.

But mostly she wondered if Cooper was right about one thing. Would she *really* have been happy as a corporate wife once Justin had stepped up and taken on a bigger role in the family business, as she knew he'd been planning to? Would she have been happy giving up her own job to support his, organising dinners and galas for him, sweet-talking potential business partners?

In truth, she was pretty sure she would have hated it.

Except that admission led her to the acknowledgement of another of Cooper's hard truths: maybe it *was* just as well Justin had jilted her.

'Are you coming?' Cooper called eventually from where he leant against Claudia's bonnet, his arms folded over his broad chest. 'I want to make Des Moines before we stop for dinner.'

Dawn absently waved a hand at him.

Des Moines could wait. She had a lot of stuff she needed to figure out first.

CHAPTER TEN

THERE WAS SOMETHING up with Dawn and, whatever it was, Cooper didn't like it.

She'd been quiet when she'd come back from the time capsule, and hadn't even objected to grabbing lunch from a drive-through to eat on the way to Des Moines. After they'd found a hotel that evening—which he'd put on his card without even thinking about it—he'd suggested dinner, but she'd declined, saying she needed some time to herself.

In Cooper's experience, that never boded well.

He'd spent the evening eating room service, avoiding the mini-bar and watching bad sci-fi movies, all while obsessing over exactly which part of what he'd said by that stupid pyramid had upset her. And, more pertinently, why he cared.

The thing was, he'd lashed out when it wasn't even her fault. He knew himself well enough to admit that talking about his ex-wife, and his abject failure of a marriage, put him in a lousy mood.

But what he couldn't tell was whether she'd been more upset at the suggestion that Justin jilting her at the altar was a good thing, or her realisation that he might be *right*.

Because he *was* right. He'd seen it in her eyes, however fast she'd tried to look away, and as much as she'd been avoiding meeting his gaze ever since.

Justin needed a wife who could play the part, like their mother had all these years. But Dawn wasn't interested in any of that.

Which led him back to his initial question— why did Justin think Dawn had been after their money? Because, as far as Cooper could tell, she wanted the perfect, romantic, true-love marriage her parents had, whether it meant being poor for life or richer than she could imagine.

And that thought just made his head hurt even more than yesterday's hangover had.

He'd hoped that the weirdness of the time capsule, and their conversations the day before, would have passed by the morning. But when

Dawn met him in the hotel lobby she was still quiet, and didn't even question his suggestion of doughnuts for breakfast again.

Yeah, he really didn't like this.

'I thought we'd stop for lunch around Walcott, Iowa,' he said, once they'd finished off the doughnuts. It was strange, he realised suddenly, how much of their day revolved around meals on this trip. Usually, he'd forget to eat at least one meal a day unless he was meeting with clients at a restaurant, or his assistant brought him something. Even then, he rarely really tasted them, distracted as he was by whatever he was working on while he ate. But on the road with Dawn he'd savoured pancakes, doughnuts, burgers, milkshakes, steaks and all sorts, and had enjoyed every mouthful.

Maybe it was the company.

No, he wasn't thinking that way. Even if he'd stayed up half the night, after the last movie had finished, with a sudden urge to put together a list of bizarre roadside attractions for them to stop off at during the rest of their journey. He'd told himself he was just being practical, but he couldn't deny that a large part of his motivation was the smile he knew Dawn would give him when they pulled off the interstate to check them out.

Oh, boy, he was in trouble.

'That sounds fine,' Dawn said, still staring out of the window. Cooper eyed her as closely as he could while still keeping his attention on the road, but didn't spot any sign that the name Walcott meant anything to her. So far, her discovery of roadside attractions had mostly seemed serendipitous, or discovered online while they'd been driving. Since she hadn't even taken her phone out of her pocket this morning, the chances were she hadn't even checked out their route for the day yet.

Good. He quite liked the idea of surprising her for a change.

He smiled to himself for the first time that morning as Claudia sped along the interstate—at least, until his mind caught up with him and started asking a whole bevy of new questions.

If Dawn was pulling away from him, it could be for two reasons, as he saw it. One, she was realising he was right and giving up any hope of a future with Justin. Which, on the off-chance that Justin *was* right about her motives, could only be a good thing. And actually, even if he wasn't, it probably wasn't exactly a *bad* one. Cooper knew his brother, and he was getting to know Dawn. They might have had the whirlwind romance but surely he was proof enough that those didn't always work out?

Of course the second reason was more troublesome. Because there was an even chance that Dawn was determined to prove him wrong instead. That she was pulling away so she could prepare herself for winning Justin back to silence the doubts that Cooper had raised.

And if that was the case he knew he couldn't let her drift too far. He had to keep her focussed on the truth—that she and Justin weren't meant to be. Not because, as his restless mind taunted him at night, the idea of watching her with his brother made his guts knot up with something he refused to call jealousy, but because it was the only way he could think of to spare Justin a messy divorce further down the line.

He never wanted his brother to have to go through the sort of heartbreak he had, whatever the cause. Dawn might not be a gold-digger—

and he still wasn't one hundred per cent certain if he could trust his gut on that—but she wasn't the right wife for Justin either. The ending would be the same, bitter one, either way.

Except that Justin loved her. Which meant, if he knew that she *wasn't* after his money, he'd want her back. So it was entirely possible Cooper was driving Dawn to a reconciliation with Justin that he was almost certain was a bad idea.

But what else could he do at this point? Apart from anything else, he wasn't willing to give up a few more days on this journey with Dawn.

Not even for his brother.

Cooper's head hurt from all the permutations and possibilities. Maybe he'd just focus on their next stop and forget all about their ultimate destination for a change.

At least, until they stopped in Chicago that night. Because then they were well over halfway to the Hamptons, and Cooper knew he had to accept that they definitely weren't turning back then. Which meant he wouldn't be able to put off a certain task any longer. Justin might have been able to ignore the text messages and emails Cooper had sent him from the road but that couldn't go on for ever.

Tonight, it was time to call his brother and warn him they were coming.

'What is it with you guys needing to be the biggest and the best?' Dawn asked as she clocked the sign at the turn-off: Walcott, Iowa, home of the World's Biggest Truck Stop. She'd known it sounded familiar when Cooper had mentioned it that morning, but she'd been too preoccupied with her own jumbled thoughts to figure out why.

'By "you guys" do you mean Americans, men or just American men?' Cooper accompanied his request for clarity with a raised eyebrow.

'A bit of all three, probably. You have to admit, it's kind of an obsession.'

'Says the woman who insisted on eating hotdogs with the world's biggest dead polar bear.' Cooper shut off the engine and opened Claudia's door. 'At least this place has a museum. About trucks.'

'A museum and all the testosterone you can

handle,' Dawn murmured as she followed him out of the car.

Cooper pointed at her across Claudia's bonnet. 'Just for that, you're driving the next leg to Chicago.'

Dawn rolled her eyes. 'I *always* drive after lunch. Because you're too grouchy to surrender the keys in the mornings—that, or you want to make sure we have the least healthy breakfast possible.' At least, that had been their routine for the past four days. Was that how long they'd been travelling together? Somehow, it seemed much longer. Wasn't time supposed to fly when you were having fun?

Because, whether she liked to admit it or not—and she didn't—Dawn *was* having fun with Cooper. Which had seemed an absolute impossibility at the start of the trip. Somehow, he was a different person out on the road.

Maybe it was Claudia's influence.

Or maybe it was hers.

Dawn shook the thought away and followed Cooper into the truck stop in search of lunch. She had a feeling they'd be trawling around every inch of the truck museum afterwards, so she wanted to be well fortified. Bypassing the chain restaurants in the food court, she headed to the Iowa 80 Kitchen, her mouth salivating at the menu. It might not be a British fish-and-chip shop, but she'd take anything that wasn't caked in sugar at the moment. One of the many things Justin had never mentioned about his brother was his sweet tooth.

As she tucked into her creamy chicken pasta *al fredo* a short while later, Dawn reflected that, while it might not be the healthiest meal ever, at least it included vegetables. She'd never before been so glad of some broccoli and mushrooms.

She surveyed Cooper over his giant burger—his third in a week, on top of the doughnuts, the pancakes, the room service and the breakfast muffins. He ate like a teenage boy, but had the body of an athletic, thirty-year-old health nut. It really wasn't fair.

'How does a workaholic like you stay in such great shape living on this sort of food?' she asked.

Cooper took an enormous bite, chewing for a long moment as he wiped ketchup from his fingers.

'I know you said you exercise,' Dawn went on, impatient at waiting for him to finish eating. 'But seriously, you'd need to be cross training for hours and hours every day to work off this stuff, and I know for a fact you'd never leave your office for that long. According to Justin, anyway.' She frowned. 'Then again, I haven't seen you working much this week either. Are you spending all night dealing with your emails?'

Cooper finally swallowed before her babbling got too much further out of hand, for which she was thankful.

'I don't normally eat like this,' he admitted, dipping one of his French fries in the sauce. 'And I haven't been working. I'm on *vacation*.'

Dawn blinked. 'Justin always said you didn't take holidays. Ever.'

'Well, then, this is my first one. My first since— Well, since my honeymoon.'

'Ah.' Wincing, Dawn looked back down at her pasta. Then across at his fries. Possibly the appeal of vegetables was wearing off.

Rolling his eyes, Cooper pushed his plate a little way across the table so she could help herself to the fries. She smiled her thanks before digging in.

'So this is your idea of a holiday, then—travelling across the country with me?' Dawn asked. 'I'd have pegged you for more of a "luxury private island in the Maldives" kind of guy.'

'That *was* my honeymoon,' Cooper admitted. 'Not something I'm particularly looking to relive.'

'I suppose I can understand that.' Although, given the chance, Dawn had to admit that the island sounded pretty damned good regardless. Except she'd probably get bored. She never had been very good at sunbathing holidays. 'Besides, there's lots more to see this way. Plenty to keep us entertained.'

'Absolutely.' The amused smile he gave her as she stole another chip suggested that *she* might be one of the more entertaining things on their trip. Well, whatever kept him paying for the hotel rooms was fine by her. They'd be sleeping in Claudia if they had to rely on her credit card for much longer.

'I was checking ahead on the route, actually,' Cooper went on. 'There's a lighthouse we could stop at tomorrow. And maybe a ghost town the next day? They're both a bit of a detour, but not too much...'

'Sounds good,' Dawn said, surprised. At the start of the trip, he'd been so desperate to get there as quickly as possible. Now he was suggesting detours? 'So, not hurrying to the Hamptons quite so much any more?'

Cooper shrugged and took another bite of his burger. 'Insert your cliché about enjoying the journey here,' he said between chews. Then he swallowed. 'Besides, if this is the only vacation I'm likely to get for a while, I might as well make the most of it, right?'

'I guess so.' Dawn smiled. 'In which case, we should totally hit the gift shop before the museum!'

That earned her a groan, but somehow Dawn sensed he wasn't quite as annoyed as he would have been four days ago.

Who would have thought it? She seemed to be growing on Cooper Edwards after all.

The truck museum, as Cooper had predicted, was wonderfully full of vintage trucks dating back to the start of the twentieth century. But, after checking them into the hotel in Chicago that night and heading to his room, he had to admit that his favourite part of their stop at Iowa 80 was watching Dawn steal his fries as they'd talked over lunch. Okay, it might also have been the very tight, bright-pink 'World's Largest Truck Stop' tee shirt she bought and insisted on wearing while she'd driven the rest of the way to Chicago.

But talking with Dawn…just talking, about vacations and lifestyle choices…reminded him how rarely he did that. Until this week.

He and Dawn had been chatting about everything and nothing since they'd made the pact to drive Claudia across the country together. But today it felt different. The conversation hadn't been as intense as the one at the time capsule, and for once she hadn't pressed with any difficult questions about his marriage or his personal life.

They'd just talked. Like friends. Like people who cared about each other.

How long had it been since he'd had someone like that in his life? Someone just to…talk to?

He shook his head as he stared down at the hotel key-card in his hand. *Too* long, that was how long.

'Cooper?' Dawn called.

He looked up along the hotel corridor and saw her standing outside her own door, just as he was outside his room. Her gaze was concerned as she watched him.

'Everything okay?' she asked.

He nodded automatically. 'Fine. I'll see you downstairs in an hour? We'll go find some dinner.'

'Sure,' Dawn said, but she still sounded uncertain. 'I'll see you there.'

Before she could ask anything else, Cooper pushed the key card into the slot and pulled it out again, the light thankfully turning green first time. Shoulder against the door, he made his way into the room, carrying his bag at his side.

It wasn't as light as it had been, he realised as he hefted it onto the bed. The bare essentials he'd bought in Sacramento four days earlier had been added to at every city and truck stop they'd broken their journey at, it seemed—as had Dawn's, he knew. In fact, her belongings were now in a cheap Des Moines-branded holdall, while his were stored in a brown leather bag he'd picked up in Salt Lake City. There hadn't seemed to be much time for shopping, but still he had a couple more outfits than he'd started with, a new book or two to read when he wasn't driving—something that annoyed Dawn a lot, since she got car sick when she tried to read in the car—and a new warm top that doubled as a dressing gown when the hotels were over-zealous with the air-con.

Basically, he'd started building up his belongings from zero again. And, while he had the funds to buy anything he chose without thinking about cost, he'd found himself choosing more carefully than he was used to. In fact, usually he just got his assistant to send out for clothes, shoes and so on from tailors and high-end stores he liked. On the road, his choices were more limited—yet he felt more satisfaction in choosing them himself than he ever had in the suit bags that arrived at his apartment from time to time.

Looking up from the bag on the bed, he was

startled by his reflection in the mirror over the desk.

He barely looked like himself. His hair was unstyled, his stubble longer than he usually kept it and the tee shirt and jeans he wore unfamiliar compared to his usual suit and tie. But it was more than that…

Cooper moved closer, peering into his own eyes in the mirror. Somehow, despite the long hours in the car, the stress of the wedding that wasn't and his ongoing uncertainty about Dawn and her motivations, he looked more relaxed than he had in years.

In fact, he might even go as far as to say he looked…happy.

He blinked, breaking the mirror's spell, and spun away. This road trip was only temporary— a week out of his real life. He couldn't afford to read too much into it, not when he had responsibilities to get back to and obligations to uphold.

Starting with his brother.

Cooper tugged his phone from his jeans pocket and hit his brother's name from his call log. He'd tried a couple of times on the wedding day but had got no answer. Since then, he'd sent a few text messages and emails asking Justin how he was, but there'd been no reply to those either.

And, for some reason, he'd never quite got round to telling his brother that he was on his way to see him. With Dawn.

Probably that was the sort of thing it would be polite to mention before they just showed up on the beach-house porch.

The phone on the other end rang and rang, and Cooper raised it to his ear just as the voicemail kicked in.

'Hi, you've reached Justin Edwards. Leave a message and I'll get back to you.'

Except Cooper knew he wouldn't. If Justin wanted to talk to him, he'd have responded to one of his messages already.

Cooper pressed the end-call button. His brother was avoiding him every bit as much as he was avoiding Dawn. Which meant that leaving a message telling him they were coming was a sure-fire way to send him running off somewhere else. Somewhere Claudia might not be able to follow. Cooper—and especially Dawn—couldn't risk that. They both needed to see Justin.

Which meant they were just going to have to surprise him.

CHAPTER ELEVEN

DAWN STARED AT her reflection in the mirror. Cooper had said they'd go somewhere nice for dinner, but the problem was she didn't really have anything in the way of nice 'going out for dinner' clothes in the meagre wardrobe she'd managed to put together over the last few days.

Sighing, she gave up pretending that the denim skirt and white tee shirt she was wearing would ever be anything approaching a slinky cocktail dress and dropped to sit down on the bed. Honestly, those people who wrote articles about the joy of capsule wardrobes had clearly never tried to look good in the same skirt for a full week, while travelling in a vintage convertible whose seats creased *everything.*

Not that it seemed to bother Cooper, who looked perfectly pressed every minute of the day regardless. And he didn't seem to care about her limited wardrobe, either. She'd assumed he just hadn't even registered her clothes—most guys she knew wouldn't have. But then she'd seen his expression when she'd put on her new 'World's Biggest Truck Stop' tee shirt...

Justin had only ever looked at her like that when she'd worn designer dresses. Cooper appeared to have tastes that were rather easier to please.

Not that she was going to read anything into it. The top had been *slightly* tighter than she'd thought it would be, that was all. Most men would have stared, right? It didn't mean anything.

Just like him letting her share his chips didn't mean anything.

Or the fact that he'd finally opened up a little bit about his wife.

All any of it meant was that they'd been spending a lot of time together and were getting to know each other. Which seemed a bit of a waste of time, now she wasn't going to marry his brother.

But somehow that didn't stop her wanting to know him even better. Or wishing she had a slinky dress to wear for dinner with him tonight.

Dawn sighed. At some point, she was going

to have to acknowledge that she might have developed a tiny bit of a crush on her ex-fiancé's brother. She was just hoping it could wait until after this road trip was over. Admitting to anything now could only make the rest of the trip excruciatingly awkward.

Either Cooper would be horrified that she was thinking about him that way when she was technically still engaged to his brother—she hadn't returned the ring yet, so she guessed it still stood—or he'd admit to feeling the same, and then what? They'd kiss, avoid each other's eyes for the next few days, she'd go and talk to his brother about their failed relationship and then she and Cooper would part ways and never see each other again.

It would have to be some kiss to make that kind of awkwardness worthwhile.

Still. Her limited wardrobe choices and ridiculous crush aside, that didn't mean she couldn't make a *bit* of an effort. It wasn't as if she got asked out to dinner in Chicago every day. Or ever before, actually.

There wasn't much she could do about her clothes, but she did dig out the gauzy, hot-pink scarf she'd picked up from the bargain bin at a convenience store attached to the diner where they'd bought doughnuts one morning. Wrapped around her neck twice, with the ends hanging loose, it at least made her boring outfit look a little more interesting.

Taking her hair down from its ponytail, she brushed it out over her shoulders, fluffing it a bit so it fell in gentle waves. With the addition of some simple make-up and the bright-pink lipstick she'd bought on a whim in Sacramento— because a girl never knew when she might need a confidence-boosting lipstick—she *almost* looked as though she might have come prepared for a night on the town.

Cooper knocked on the door moments later, and Dawn steeled herself before opening it. What had it come to that she had to prepare herself for seeing him, knowing that if he looked too good he'd take her breath away? She felt like a teenager with a first crush, rather than a woman who'd been through the relationship mill too many times to count.

Maybe that was the appeal. She knew anything with Cooper could never be a relationship—he hated the idea of marriage and she'd already been engaged to his brother, for heaven's sake—and that made him safe. She could lust from afar, flirt over chips, have fancy dinners out and never worry about it meaning a thing.

She grinned to herself as she pulled open the door. Maybe she'd do exactly that.

'Wow,' Cooper said, eyebrows raised. 'You look…'

'Exactly like I've done every other day of this trip?' Dawn finished for him. 'Because I still haven't got round to buying a second skirt.'

'I was going to say great. Or beautiful. Or something better than that.' Cooper's gaze seemed to be fixed on her lips.

Score one for the lipstick.

But her moment of triumph faded as she took in his appearance. He hadn't dressed up much either, for the same obvious reason, but still the jeans that moulded so perfectly to his legs, the collared tee-shirt that highlighted his throat and those broad, broad shoulders, the stubble that made him look just that little bit more devil-may-care than she'd ever imagined he could… all added up to a truly delectable picture.

One that really made her want to smudge her lipstick.

But, no. Flirting. Dinner. Fun. That was all.

Anything else could never end well.

She just had to keep reminding herself of that.

'Shall we go?' she asked, smiling brightly. And hoping against hope that she could hold off kissing her fiancé's brother until they hit the Hamptons.

Dinner was a hit. As he'd predicted, Dawn loved the steak place he'd picked for them to eat at, happily trying everything he suggested, as well as everything he'd ordered for himself.

'I spent too long eating boring food,' she explained after moaning around a mouthful of steak and sauce béarnaise. 'I'm making up for it.'

Simply watching her eat, those bright-pink lips closing around her fork, was making Cooper hungry. Just not for food.

He was hungry for her company, her conversation—the easy way they tossed thoughts and comments back and forth without needing to read too much into them.

Although he had to admit he might have

missed some of what she was saying because he was too busy staring at her lips. Imagining how it would feel to kiss them. To be fair, though, Dawn had trailed off a few times mid-sentence too. Which only made things worse, because he was almost certain she was imagining the same things he was.

Which meant he was in really big trouble.

He wanted her.

He wanted his little brother's fiancée in a way he hadn't wanted anyone since the ex-wife who'd broken his heart and taken half his fortune.

And he knew the only reason Justin had called things off was because he thought Dawn was a gold-digger—something Cooper was almost certain wasn't the case. In which case...he had to take Dawn back to his brother. Give them another chance at happiness together.

Except they were wrong for each other, damn it! Having spent four days talking to her, and a lifetime knowing Justin, he could tell that instantly. She wouldn't be happy with him, and he'd want her to be things she wasn't. Or at least, things that didn't come naturally to her.

Justin was a caviar-and-champagne guy. He

always had to have the most expensive of everything, just because it cost more.

Dawn, he'd established, appreciated the *best* things, whatever the cost.

No, Cooper was absolutely convinced that Dawn and Justin together would be a mistake.

The only problem with that was that he was hugely, ridiculously biased, and he knew it.

What if he only saw these problems because he wanted them to be true? Because he wanted Dawn for himself? He'd only seen them together as a couple for twenty-four hours before Justin had run out. What did he know about their life together? Maybe Justin was a different guy with Dawn.

Cooper sure as hell was.

After he'd paid the bill, they'd walked the few blocks back to the hotel, talking about nothing at all. And it wasn't until they reached her room that Cooper admitted to himself quite how much he didn't want the night to end.

'So, we'll meet in the lobby as normal?' Dawn asked, leaning against her door as she smiled up at him.

'Yeah. Say, nine?' Cooper hoped he managed

to sound normal and unaffected by her presence. He definitely didn't feel it.

It wasn't her clothes, or her hair, make-up or even the soft scent of whatever products she'd been using that filled his lungs and made him want. It wasn't even the conversation. It was her smile—the easy, happy, optimistic smile that told him that she didn't want to be anywhere else, that she didn't need anything from him, that she was just happy to be there.

That was the part that was going to ruin him.

'Goodnight, Dawn.' Leaning down, he brushed a swift kiss against her cheek, then turned away, heading back to his own room.

He needed sleep. And he needed to move past this strange connection he'd forged with his brother's fiancée.

Even if he had no idea how to do that.

And even if he knew he would spend all night dreaming about pink lipstick—and *wanting*.

'So, tell me about this lighthouse of yours,' Dawn said as Chicago faded away into the background through Claudia's back window.

Cooper had beaten her down to the lobby that

morning for the first time all week, and had been waiting for her with warm and gooey cheese and ham croissants—always the sign of an excellent day, in her book. Following on from a great evening the night before, as it happened.

Dawn was glad she had picked out her bright-pink 'truck stop' tee shirt to wear again that morning. From the way Cooper's eyes roamed over the logo on it, she figured it was basically a thank-you in clothing form for the croissant.

'I wouldn't call it *my* lighthouse,' Cooper said with the nonchalance of a man who might actually own a lighthouse somewhere. His family certainly had the money, and Dawn had never been able to keep all their property straight in her head.

'You were the one who wanted to stop there,' she pointed out. 'So what's so great about it?'

Cooper shrugged, glancing away from the road to look at her. 'I just saw a picture on the Internet and figured you might like it, was all.'

A warm feeling flowed through her at his casual words. However bad an idea her crush was, at least after the last day or so she was almost certain that Cooper returned it. Maybe they'd never be able to act on it, but just knowing that he'd picked out a place to visit because he thought she'd like it went a long way to making her feel a little better about the whole situation.

'It's still a good four hours' drive, though,' Cooper added. 'If you wanted to get some sleep?'

'Are you saying I look tired?' she asked, eyebrows raised. Admittedly, her night's rest had been punctuated by more dreams of him than she was willing to admit to, but Dawn didn't think it was anything her concealer hadn't hid. But, as she looked at him, she realised that *Cooper* looked exhausted. As if he hadn't slept all night.

As if he'd been as disturbed by dreams and imaginings as she had.

Huh.

'You look full of the joys of summer, as always,' Cooper said with a mocking smile that suddenly didn't seem so mocking.

'Do you want me to drive?' she asked bluntly. 'I mean, if you need to sleep, I can drive to the lighthouse. You can take over afterwards.'

She could see common sense warring with pride in his expression. Clearly he was too exhausted to drive safely, but he was also equally unwilling to admit it.

So Dawn made the decision for him. 'Pull over.'

'I don't need you to—'

'And I don't plan to die in a car accident before making it to the Hamptons, thanks. So pull over and we can swap seats.' She stared at him until he did as she asked.

Dawn climbed out of Claudia's passenger side first, moving swiftly around to the other side to open Cooper's door for him. As he got out, he held her arm gently to stop her sliding into his vacated seat.

'Thanks,' he said softly, his mouth so close to her cheek she could feel his breath. 'I…didn't sleep much last night.'

'Bad dreams?' She stared up into his eyes as she asked and watched his pupils grow wide and black.

'Quite the opposite, actually.' Cooper's voice, rough, low and dark, rang through her body until she felt as though every cell of it was vibrating at the sound.

God, she wanted him. And it looked as though he wanted her every bit as much.

She swallowed and looked away, fumbling for the steering wheel as she climbed into her seat.

'We should get going,' she said.

Cooper nodded, making his way round to the passenger seat. 'Long way to the lighthouse,' he agreed.

And an even longer way to the Hamptons. And her ex-fiancé.

When Cooper awoke again, Dawn was singing along to Elvis on the radio—it seemed to be the only music Claudia would consent to play—and they were just passing a sign for Marblehead Lighthouse State Park. Dawn's phone was set to the sat nav app, and calling out periodic directions.

'How long was I out?' He straightened up in his seat, rubbing at the back of his neck to try and ease the ache there.

'Felt like for ever,' Dawn quipped as she turned onto a smaller road. 'Any more dreams?'

The look she gave him told him that she had a pretty good idea what his dreams had been about. Hardly surprising, given the heat that had radiated between them when he'd told her the reason he hadn't slept.

Thankfully, he'd been too exhausted to dream during his car nap, because otherwise things could have got very awkward, very fast.

'Totally dreamless,' he said with relief.

'Glad to hear it,' Dawn replied, although her tone said something different.

Did she *want* him to dream about her? Had she been dreaming about him?

Cooper stared out of the window and bit back a curse. Apparently, ignoring the attraction between them wasn't working any longer—if it ever had.

Which meant they were going to have to talk about it.

Damn.

Dawn parked and together they made their way into the state park, both stretching as they walked to work out the kinks that four-plus hours in a car gave a person.

On the shores of Lake Erie, the park was strangely peaceful, even in the summer high season. As they followed the trail towards the shore, the red-tipped lighthouse, white except for its cap and the red railings lower down, stood proudly against the water. He'd read something about tours, Cooper thought vaguely, and about climbing the steps to the top of the lighthouse and looking out. But he was content just to look at it from the outside. To soak up the atmosphere and the calm of the lake and park.

To relax, for once.

At least, until Dawn said, 'So, are we going to talk about it?'

It was just like pulling off a sticking plaster, Dawn reasoned. Obviously there was something between them—something distracting, awkward and potentially difficult. The sooner they talked about it, the sooner they could move on.

Even if her heart was pounding in her chest as she asked.

'Talk about what?' Cooper asked, his expression blank. Then he sighed. 'Never mind. I know what.'

He sank down to sit on a nearby bench, the summer sun glinting off his dark hair, and his legs stretched out in front of him as he stared down at his hands.

Dawn perched beside him, her own hands clasped too tightly in her lap as she tried to figure out what she wanted to say.

Cooper beat her to it. 'Here's the thing—I don't have friends. I never really noticed until this week, but I don't. I have colleagues and business contacts, maybe even a few acquaintances I know well enough to meet for a drink if I'm in town. But not friends. Not until this week.'

'You think we're friends?' Dawn asked, surprised.

'I think we could be.' Cooper looked up at last, meeting her eyes, and she almost gasped at the sincerity in them. 'I think that spending this week with you in that stupid car, stopping at ridiculous roadside attractions and eating junk food for every meal, has been the most fun I've had in years.'

'You need to get out more. Meet more people,' Dawn joked, but Cooper didn't laugh.

'Maybe you're right. Maybe it is time to get back out there. Meet people.' And by 'people' Dawn assumed he meant women.

In fact, he sounded as if the thought was a revelation. As if he'd just realised a universal truth—probably the same one men had been realising all through her life.

Dawn's spirits took a nose dive. Talk about backsliding. Her last relationship had made it all the way to the altar, even if it hadn't got any further. This one—if you could even call it a relationship—hadn't even made it to the first kiss.

'The thing is, I don't think it's *people*,' Cooper said. 'I think it's you.'

Dawn jerked her head up to stare at him. 'Me?' It was never *her*. That was the point.

Cooper nodded. 'Because I meet people every day, Dawn. And I don't let them in. I don't want to let them in. I didn't want to let *you* in.'

'I kind of got that.'

'But you got there anyway. And maybe that's just forced proximity in Claudia.'

'You're making this sound like a sort of Stockholm Syndrome friendship here,' Dawn pointed out.

'Or maybe it's just you,' Cooper finished as if she hadn't spoken. 'But the thing is, Dawn, I'm a different person with you. And I like him a lot more than the person I've been since Rachel left me.'

Rachel. So that was his ex-wife's name.

'So…me and this new you,' Dawn said cautiously. 'We're…friends?'

'Yes,' Cooper said, but there was something in his voice. A note of uncertainty, maybe. Something she couldn't quite place until he added, 'Except I keep dreaming about your pink lipstick.'

Score two for Flamingo Shimmer.

'My lipstick?'

When had he got so close? One moment they were sitting beside each other on the bench, a perfectly respectable distance between them, and now…now she could almost feel the warmth of his skin in the sunshine as his arm brushed close to hers and his lips moved closer.

'Uh huh. I keep imagining how it would feel to kiss you. Dreaming of it, in fact.'

'Just…kissing?' Dawn asked, because apparently she didn't know when just to go with a good thing.

'No,' Cooper admitted. 'Not just kissing.'

And then, before she could even process that thought, Cooper leant in that extra inch and suddenly his lips were on hers, warm and soft and perfect, just as she'd imagined.

Until they were gone again, far too soon.

'I shouldn't have done that.' Cooper pushed away against the floor until he was sat at the far end of the bench.

'I beg to differ.' Dawn said, her lips still tingling.

'You're engaged to my brother.'

'He left me at the altar,' Dawn pointed out. 'I think that's a pretty clear sign that it's over.'

'Then why are we chasing him across the country?' Cooper raised his eyebrows as he waited for an answer.

Dawn stared at him in amazement. 'Oh, my God. You think I'm going to beg Justin to take me back!'

'Well, aren't you?'

'No!' Dawn said, but honesty compelled her to add, 'Maybe I might have wanted to, at first. Just a bit. But that's not why we're on this road trip. It's not what you think.'

'Then explain it to me. Please.'

It wasn't a story that Dawn really wanted to

tell, but the brief flare of hope that shone in Cooper's eyes told her she needed to.

'Okay. But not here. Come on, we need to get Claudia back on the road if we want to stop in Cleveland tonight.'

She stood and held out a hand to Cooper. After a moment, he took it. And somehow, as they walked to the car, he never quite let go.

CHAPTER TWELVE

'Do you know what my sisters call me?' Dawn asked as Claudia pulled out of the Marblehead Lighthouse State Park.

Cooper glanced across at her in surprise. Given their previous conversation, this was not where he'd imagined their talk going next.

'Dawn, I'd assume,' he said flippantly.

'They call me the Dry Run.' There was pain in Dawn's voice—pain he wanted to kiss away, if only he hadn't been driving. But, for the life of him, he couldn't figure out what the nickname meant.

'I don't get it.'

'Every guy I've ever dated—and I do mean every single one,' she clarified, leaving him wondering exactly how many there had been. 'Every guy I've ever been out with has left me then gone on to meet the love of his life and marry them within the next two years.'

Cooper blinked. Suddenly the number seemed more relevant than just calming his sudden jealous spurt. If it had been one or two guys, that might be put down to coincidence. But more…

'How many boyfriends are we talking here? For statistical reasons only, I promise,' he added, when she started to object.

'Five,' Dawn answered. 'Six if you count Billy Nolan, which I suppose we could.'

'Billy Nolan?'

'We were ten, so the marriage part took a little longer. But the next month a new girl moved to town and they were sweethearts all through secondary school and university, and got married the day after graduation.'

'Six men. Six different men seriously passed you up to marry someone else?' The words were out before he could think about their implication, but the pink tinge on Dawn's cheeks told him she didn't much mind.

'I'm the girl guys date for years, knowing it's not everything they ever dreamed of but thinking it might be enough—until they find the real thing and they realise I could never compare.'

Okay, now he understood that pain. The bitter

ache he heard in her words. The crushing feeling of never being enough, of not measuring up. Of being a fool for ever thinking you could. He knew *exactly* how that felt, and he hated that Dawn had ever had to experience it once, let alone six times. It made him wonder how she could possibly keep picking herself back up and trying again. How she could keep that unflagging optimism.

But the one thing he couldn't help but notice she *hadn't* said was that she didn't want Justin back. She might not plan to beg, but that wasn't the same as not wanting.

He wouldn't press her. But he wouldn't ignore it either. And he knew he couldn't kiss her again, not as he had by the lighthouse anyway, without knowing her intentions towards his brother. Knowing if she still loved him.

Which meant they were on hold. But they were still friends, and suddenly he wanted to give some of that friendship back to her.

'Rachel cheated on me on our honeymoon,' he said, without really knowing why. Maybe he just wanted to offer her something of his own pain to balance things out.

He saw Dawn wince out of the corner of his eye, and kept talking just to stop himself having to hear her inevitable sympathy and pity.

'In fairness, she'd been cheating on me all through our engagement too,' he said. 'And I didn't actually find out until we'd been married a month or so. Turns out that the whole fidelity part of marriage had passed her by entirely.'

Dawn shook her head. 'I don't understand. Why would she do that? How could she?'

Because all she wanted me for was my name, my lifestyle and, most of all, my money.

But that truth still hurt too much to share, to know that his entire worth could be numbered in dollars and still be found lacking.

'We had different expectations from marriage, I guess,' he said instead. 'She wanted someone who would pay for the lifestyle she wanted— who would get her into the parties and places she thought she belonged in. Someone who could give her prestige and position and the money to do anything she wanted. And I could give her all of that, of course. In return, I just wanted her love, but apparently that part wasn't for sale.'

'I'm so sorry.'

'It was years ago now,' Cooper said, trying to brush her pity aside. He didn't need it. 'And at least she taught me an important lesson about people.'

'Which is?'

'You can never know another person fully. Not really.' Cooper's realised his knuckles were white where he gripped the steering wheel, and tried to loosen his hold. 'The best you can try and do is know yourself.'

'And do you?' Dawn asked. 'Know yourself, I mean?'

Cooper looked across at her. 'I always thought I did,' he said, softly. 'Until I met you.'

'We still need to talk about that kiss,' Dawn reminded Cooper as they stopped outside their adjoining motel rooms in Cleveland that night. She'd had a text from her credit card provider with the news that her limit increase had been approved, so she'd insisted on paying again. Of course, that meant they were in a cheap motel on the edge of the city with doors that faced out onto the car park and a cheap porch covering overhead—because the increase wasn't *that* much—but she still felt better for being able to pay her way.

Even if the walls were so thin she'd probably be able to hear Cooper snoring that night. Or if he called out anything in his sleep.

Like maybe her name…

'We do.' Cooper sounded exhausted and he leant against the wooden doorframe as he spoke. The second part of the day's driving—which should have only taken another hour or so—had ended up taking three, thanks to a pile-up on the interstate. They'd stopped and eaten a silent, exhausted dinner on the way into town so they wouldn't have to leave the motel again once they were checked in.

He looked absolutely ready to drop, and here she was asking him to have a deep and meaningful conversation about their feelings.

No wonder men left her.

'It'll keep,' she said, with a smile she didn't feel. 'We can talk tomorrow.'

'That might be best.' Cooper's answering smile had more than a little relief in it. 'I have a feeling it's not the sort of conversation you'd thank me for falling asleep during.'

'Probably not.' She slipped her key into the door and opened it, turning back to say, 'Goodnight, Cooper.'

To her surprise, he leant forward and pressed another soft kiss to her lips. 'Goodnight, Dawn. Sweet dreams.' Then he was gone into his room, the door shutting firmly behind him.

Dawn stood staring after him all the same. Somehow, she had a feeling that her dreams that night would be anything but sweet.

Especially when she opened her own door and found a naked stranger in the middle of the room.

Ten minutes later, Dawn had established three things. One: that the new app they were using to book hotels since the disaster with the one in Salt Lake City also sucked, since it had let her book two rooms in a motel where there was apparently only one free room. Two: the girl running the reception desk at this motel didn't much care for her problems. And three: she was far too tired even to think about finding anywhere else to stay that night.

Her eyes itching with tiredness, Dawn leant

outside Cooper's bedroom door and tried to work up the courage to knock. What was the worst he could do? Send her to sleep in Claudia instead?

Even that sounded preferable to being awake for another moment. And it might even be more comfortable than the couch in Salt Lake City.

Raising her hand, she knocked lightly on the door, hoping she wouldn't wake him.

'Dawn?' Cooper answered it wearing just a pair of shorts, his dark hair even messier than normal and his eyes barely open. 'What's going on? Are you okay?'

'I think we're actually cursed,' she said. 'I can't believe it happened again.'

'What happened again?' Cooper frowned, and she saw the moment he got it. 'Oh.'

'Yeah. The stupid motel overbooked,' she explained. 'My room is already occupied by an alarmingly naked old guy, and there aren't any others free. Can I crash in here with you tonight? I'll even take the couch again.'

Cooper's eyes widened at that, and Dawn was suddenly all too aware that this wasn't like last time. Last time, he hadn't kissed her just that afternoon. Last time, she hadn't even imagined that she could want him to do it again.

And it suddenly occurred to her that this could look like something it wasn't.

'I swear this isn't a play, Cooper. There really aren't any other rooms. And to be honest, I don't think either of us has the energy to make this into anything tonight anyway.' If they couldn't even stay awake long enough to *talk* about the kiss, what were the chances of it happening again before either of them got any sleep?

Cooper didn't answer, so Dawn reached down to pick up her bag again and stepped back. 'Never mind. I'll sleep in the car.'

'No!' His hand shot out at that, grabbing her wrist and tugging her towards him. 'Sorry. I'm just half-asleep. Of course you can stay here. And you don't have to take the couch. Not least because there isn't one.'

He let her go, running a hand through his hair as he stepped aside to let her into the room.

There wasn't much of it, she realised. What with the naked guy next door, she hadn't taken in much of the room she'd originally been as-signed, but it was clear now that they'd got what she'd paid for: not much. A double bed, barely more than a single, a small table with a kettle and mug on it, with some instant coffee sachets, a TV on the wall and presumably a bathroom through the other door on the far side.

Absolute basic, minimum-requirement motel room.

'We could go find somewhere else to stay,' she suggested, looking back at the very small bed. 'If you'd rather.'

Cooper covered his mouth as he gave a jaw-cracking yawn. 'Dawn, it's late. We're both exhausted. We can share. Come on. Let's go to bed.'

She nodded, hoping this wasn't the worst idea she'd ever had. Although it wasn't as if it didn't have some stiff competition.

It was strange, getting ready for bed in the bathroom, knowing that Cooper was just in the next room, already under the covers. The covers they needed to share. God, what if he was a blanket hog?

And she still hadn't bought any pyjamas. Damn. It hadn't been such a problem last time, when she could wrap a blanket round herself for full coverage.

Pulling out the longest of her collection of tee shirts, she pulled it on, leaving her knickers on with it and hoping for the best. Like he'd said, they were both too tired to think, let alone have inappropriate thoughts about each other. This would be fine. Two friends sharing a bed. That was all.

No problem.

She tried to smile at herself in the mirror, but even her reflection seemed to know that she was lying.

Well, no point putting it off. Dawn finished cleaning her teeth then turned off the bathroom light, heading back into the bedroom.

Cooper lay on the far side of the bed, his back turned towards her, the covers pulled up to his waist and his torso bare. Dawn gave herself precisely fifteen seconds to enjoy the view before she slipped into the bed beside him, her back to his, and pulled up the sheets to cover her. Reaching out, she switched off the light and lay, eyes open, in the darkness.

'Goodnight, Dawn,' Cooper murmured without moving.

'Goodnight.' The bed wasn't particularly soft, but it was better than Claudia's back seat. And the blankets might be scratchy, but they were keeping her from touching Cooper's skin and losing her mind.

All she had to do now was remember how to sleep, when Cooper was lying next to her half-naked.

Yep. Absolutely no problem at all.

Cooper hadn't expected to sleep from the moment Dawn had showed up at his door, roomless and bed-less for the night. Just the idea of trying to pass out while she was curled up beside him seemed impossible.

But it turned out that complete and utter exhaustion had its benefits.

The only problem was, he slept *too* well, and woke up fully rested at six the next morning.

Wrapped around Dawn's sleeping body.

Cooper froze as he came suddenly and completely awake. Okay, this was bad. They still hadn't talked about that kiss, he still didn't know if she still loved Justin, he still hadn't figured out if he should even tell her about his brother's suspicions…and here he was, every inch of his body pressed against hers. And damn him if he didn't want to get even closer.

No. Not like this.

It took all his willpower to carefully unravel their closeness, his jaw set and tense as he eased his way out of the bed without waking her.

He needed to figure out all kinds of things before he could be that close to Dawn again, and he wasn't sure his resolve would last if she woke up and blinked those big eyes at him. If she smiled. If she kissed him again…

Damn it. He needed to stop.

With a shuddering breath, and one last look at the woman asleep in his bed, Cooper went to find a very cold shower. And hopefully some more willpower.

Dawn woke alone, and had showered away the vague sense of regret about that and managed to get dressed before Cooper returned to the room fully clothed and with breakfast in his hand.

'We should get going,' he said, not looking at her directly.

So. It was going to be like that.

'I'm ready when you are,' she said as she brushed past him towards where they'd parked Claudia the night before.

And she meant it. Sooner or later, they'd have to talk.

Although apparently, if Cooper had his way, it would be later. Much, much later.

Usually, their conversation was sparse in the mornings as Cooper slowly worked his way out of the bad mood he always seemed to wake up in. But today, he was full of things to say—keeping her distracted from the conversation they weren't having by instigating all sorts of other ones instead.

Dawn played along. For now.

By the time Cooper pulled into a roadside diner for lunch, she had learned all sorts of new things about her road-trip companion. His favourite colours, favourite Elvis song, his most annoying habits—which his assistant had alphabetised—least favourite airports...and many more. But nothing on the one subject she was interested in.

That kiss.

She didn't think he was regretting it, exactly, but he was pulling away all the same. Filling the distance between them with minutiae and top-ten lists.

Well, he wasn't going to get away with that for ever.

Caroline's Diner was just like any of the others they'd stopped in over the last five days or so: red seats and white tables, jukebox in the corner, burgers on the menu. But this lunch didn't feel anything like the same.

'So, what are your favourite burger toppings?' Cooper asked, already hidden behind the menu, and Dawn knew it was time to call him out.

'Cooper. Stop.'

'Stop what?' His dark-brown eyes appeared over the top of the menu, trying too hard to look innocent.

Dawn sighed. 'Look, if you're regretting the kiss, or even last night... If you want to forget that it ever happened—'

'No! I don't. Really.' Dropping the menu to the

table, he reached out and placed his hand over hers. 'Really, Dawn.'

'Then what's with the constant games of twenty questions, when none of the questions are anything either of us actually care about?'

Cooper pulled a face. 'I guess I don't… I don't know how to do this.' He gestured between them.

'What, hold an actual conversation?'

'About our feelings? Basically.'

She laughed. Of course he didn't. The man didn't have any friends.

'I figured if I just kept talking, eventually I'd say the right things just by sheer probability theory.' He shrugged. 'Of course, there was the chance I'd say all the wrong ones first.'

'Not wrong. Just irrelevant.'

'Is it, though?' Cooper tilted his head as he stared across the table at her. 'I mean, we agreed we were friends. Friends know this stuff about each other, right?'

'I suppose so,' Dawn allowed. 'But is friends what we're still going for here?' Because those kisses had said otherwise. As had her rather spicy dreams the night before. In fact she was almost certain she'd woken in the middle of the night to feel his arms wrapped around her before she'd drifted off again...

Cooper looked away. 'Dawn, you're still engaged to my brother. And I know he left you, but he had reasons, and I can't get between the two of you until you sort things out.'

Of course. It all came back to Justin. How was he still screwing her over even *after* he'd jilted her?

'Your brother left me at the altar,' she pointed out. 'Trust me when I tell you that even I, Miss Dry Run herself, has more self-respect than to chase after a man who has made it so abundantly clear he doesn't want to marry me.'

Cooper raised his eyebrows at her and gestured to Claudia. 'Then care to explain to me what the last five days have been about?'

She supposed he had a point. It did look rather a lot like they were chasing Justin across the country.

Dawn took a deep breath. 'I'm not going to talk to Justin to win him back.'

'Or to reclaim your passport or belongings,

I assume, since he could have easily have arranged to courier them back to you by now.'

She winced as she remembered the lame excuses she'd made that first night. She should have known he'd see through them.

'No. Although I do want them back.' Dawn tried to find the right words to explain, and settled on the one Ruby had used that first night. 'I'm not chasing Justin. I'm chasing closure.'

'Closure?'

'Yeah.' He wasn't getting it, she could see. 'This time, I need to know why. I need to know what it is about me that isn't good enough for anyone to want "forever" with me. I need to understand what I did wrong.'

'What *you* did wrong?' Cooper asked. 'Sweetheart, you remember that *he* was the one who stood you up on your wedding day, right?'

Dawn sighed, searching for a way to make him understand. 'When you found out that Rachel was cheating, did you ask her why?'

'No.' Cooper shifted in his seat as he said the word, looking uncomfortable.

'Well, maybe you should have done. It might have helped you move on sooner if you understood her reasons.' Although, to be honest, Dawn could only assume insanity. Had the woman even *seen* Cooper? Who the hell had she thought she was going to find who was better than Cooper Edwards madly in love with her?

'Her reasons were that she was an untrustworthy, lying, cheating—'

'Those aren't *her* reasons,' Dawn interrupted. 'They're your interpretations. Like me saying that Justin is a twisted, cruel man for jilting me.'

'Dawn, I know my brother isn't perfect, but he's not cruel. Usually.'

'I know,' Dawn said simply. 'And that's why I need to see him. To understand what made him act that way.'

'I suppose that makes sense,' Cooper allowed. 'But what happens next? When you have your closure?'

'I move on.' Just the thought of it made her smile. 'I start the rest of my life. But first, I need to exorcise all my ghosts about every guy who ever left me and went off to find his true love. I need to let it all go.'

Cooper smirked. 'In that case, you're going to love our next stop. Come on. I'm driving.'

CHAPTER THIRTEEN

COOPER WASN'T ENTIRELY sure what he'd been expecting from a ghost town, but it hadn't been this.

The highway petered out as they approached, the road becoming cracked and uneven. Grass grew between bits of tarmac, and he thought he could even see a strange wisp of steam rising from between one of the cracks.

Uneasy, he pulled Claudia over to the side of the road and cut the engine. He had a feeling the car wouldn't enjoy exploring the town ahead.

'It says on this website that there's been a fire raging underground here for over fifty years,' Dawn whispered, staring at the road ahead rather than the phone in her hand. 'The fumes are toxic, so I guess we'd better not get too close to those cracks.'

Cooper reached for Claudia's keys again. 'Okay, maybe this wasn't such a good idea. We

can just exorcise our ghosts the way normal people do—with alcohol and bad choices.'

But Dawn was already climbing out of the car.
'No. I want to see it. I want to do this.'

Well. It wasn't as though he could let her go
alone, so...

Locking Claudia behind them, Cooper followed her along the road into what remained of
the town of Centralia.

'It used to be a mining community,' Dawn
told him as they walked. He smiled to himself.
It might have been his idea to come here but, as
usual, it was Dawn who'd read up on all the details and memorised them. 'There were fifteen
hundred people living here once.'

'So what happened?' He'd already read the
website himself, but somehow it felt more real
when Dawn told him the story.

'They think the fire started in a rubbish dump
over a coal seam,' she said. 'Firefighters tried
to put it out, but the fire clung to the coal and
went underground. It's been burning up the earth
under the town ever since, making everything
unstable. Including Graffiti Highway.'

She gestured to the road in front of them, and

Cooper saw instantly what she meant. The whole road was covered in street art spray-painted on the crumbling road, a riot of colours and designs.

'Graffiti artists come from all over to paint here, even though they know it could collapse at any time.' Dawn sounded bemused by the idea.

'I guess some people like living on the edge. Taking chances.' He couldn't help but stare at her as he said it, though, instead of the road.

'Do you?' she asked, looking up to meet his gaze.

'I never thought I did,' he answered honestly. 'But this week… A little risk-taking doesn't seem like the worst thing in the world.'

Her smile told him she knew he wasn't only talking about exploring a volatile ghost town.

Cooper reached for her hand as they wandered up the highway to a small graveyard—one of three in the town, according to Dawn's research. Cooper let her words wash over him as she told him about the residents who wouldn't leave, and how the town had been shut down in pieces. It was interesting, of course, but none of it seemed to matter as much as being there with *her*.

She wasn't trying to win Justin back. She was

ready to move on. She hadn't told him she wasn't still in love with Justin, of course, but it was a start. No, it was more than that. It was something he hadn't felt in a long time. Hope.

Maybe all he'd take away from this road trip in the end was memories of the person he'd been. But maybe, just maybe, he could keep something more.

Dawn.

'Are you ready to go back to the car?' she asked as they looked out over the small graveyard. The eerie stillness of the place sent a shiver down his back but, even though every inch of him was itching to get away, he made himself stand there a moment longer.

'That depends. Have you exorcised those ghosts?' he asked.

Dawn tilted her head to the side. 'I think so. This town…it's desolate. Everyone—or almost everyone—has abandoned it and left it. But it's still beautiful, in its own way. And one day, maybe that fire will stop burning. Maybe life can return here.'

Was she describing the place or herself? He hoped it was the former. Although, he had to admit, he felt a sense of kinship with Centralia as she described it. As if he were the town, and the fire burning the place up from the inside was Rachel's and Melanie's betrayals, and everything that had ever made him feel like he couldn't trust the world.

Maybe it was time to put that fire out at last.

Time to feel something again.

Maybe even love.

'Then let's go.' Cooper tugged on Dawn's hand and led her back towards Claudia. He hoped her ghosts were gone.

But he knew for certain he was leaving his own behind in this ghost town.

Dawn shuddered a little as she pulled Claudia away from Centralia and back towards the interstate. The town had been interesting, if creepy, but the most fascinating part to her had been how Cooper had reacted to the place.

She didn't mind that he clearly hadn't been listening too attentively as she'd given him her best tour-guide impression, because he'd obviously been lost in thought. He'd taken her hand again, and kept hold of it as they walked, as if that were just normal for them, now. Better still, she'd actually been able to see his expression turning lighter, his shoulders relaxing.

Odd as it sounded, something about that eerie, toxic, abandoned town had let Cooper release something. She hoped it might be his past.

'We should make it to New York tonight,' Cooper said as the more familiar landscape of the I-80 surrounded them once more. 'What do you want to do then?'

'What are my options?' she asked.

'Well, we could carry on, arrive at the beach house late tonight and bring this whole road trip to a close.' He left that hanging there, obviously waiting to see how she liked it.

Dawn's nose wrinkled up. She didn't like it very much at all, as it happened. 'Or?'

'Or we could stay in New York and have a night on the town before we go get you your closure.'

'I suppose it would be better to arrive in the morning than late at night,' she said, giving him a small smile.

He returned it. 'Closure does work better when you're well rested, I've heard.'

'Plus it would just be rude to arrive so late,' Dawn went on.

'Exactly.' Cooper grinned. 'I guess I'd better find us somewhere to stay, then.'

He pulled up the familiar hotel app on his phone, and Dawn bit her bottom lip, forcing herself to keep her eyes on the road and not on his phone screen.

Not even to check if he was booking two hotel rooms or just one.

They switched driving again when they stopped for coffee in New Jersey, and as night started to fall Cooper drove them through the Holland tunnel and into the bright lights of New York City.

'Where are we staying?' she asked as they stuttered through the stop-start city traffic.

'You'll see,' was all Cooper would say.

She assumed he'd have booked one of the more famous hotels, mostly because she knew he liked quality. Which was why she was surprised when he pulled into a small, private parking garage right next to Central Park.

'Where are we?' she asked as he cut the engine.

He flashed her a smile. 'Home sweet home.'

'You have an apartment in New York.' Of course he did. How had she not remembered that before?

'I do.' He reached out across the seats and took her hand. 'Care to stay here with me tonight? I can book you a hotel, if you'd rather. I did look, but given the luck we've had with that booking app lately… I figured, if we had to share a bed, I'd rather it be mine.'

She saw the real question in his eyes and swallowed hard. This wouldn't be like last night—awkward distances and pretending to sleep until her body overcame her mind and she passed out. This wouldn't be two friends sharing a bed out of necessity.

This would be them. Together.

Tomorrow they'd be with Justin. She'd find her closure and be ready to move on—to go and find her own future. And Cooper… Well, he was ready to find love again, she was certain. But it couldn't be with her.

'Just for tonight?' She met his gaze and saw understanding there.

This couldn't be anything more. They both still had healing to do to move on from their past relationships. Not to mention the fact that family gatherings would be *beyond* awkward. And hadn't he been the one to point out that she'd never be happy living the life of the corporate wife he—and Justin—both needed?

For once, Dawn was stepping into something without thinking about forever. Tonight wouldn't lead to a white dress and a happily ever after. When it was over, she'd still be the same Dawn she'd always been, the Dry Run. And Cooper... He'd do what men always did after they left her—find the love of his life.

She could give him that.

She'd take one night of pleasure in his arms then set him free to find his happy ending.

And maybe, just maybe, she'd find hers one day too.

But until then she was going to enjoy the moment, for a change.

'Just for tonight,' Cooper murmured back to her, the air thick between them.

Dawn smiled. 'Then lead the way.'

'I can still take you out for that fancy night on the town, if you like?' Cooper offered as he pushed open his front door. How long had it been since he'd been back to his New York place? It couldn't have been more than a month or so, before the Europe trip and the wedding that wasn't. But somehow it felt much longer, as though he was a different person, now he was here again.

Or maybe it was just that he wasn't used to being here with company.

He dropped Claudia's keys and his own into the bowl on the kitchen counter, and ignored the stack of mail sitting next to it. His housekeeping staff in the building kept the place in good shape while he was away, and he knew anything of importance would already have been forwarded to the office.

'Maybe…it might be nice to actually spend a quiet night in, for once,' Dawn said, a soft, promising smile on her face.

Did she know what that look in her eyes did to him? The one that told him that whatever she had in mind for him wouldn't be all that quiet?

Probably not, which might actually be why he found it so damn appealing.

He could see how Justin had fallen for her all too easily. What he still couldn't understand was how his brother had come to the conclusion that Dawn was a gold-digger. Everything he'd learned about her over the last week had showed him a different person altogether.

A woman he'd fallen for, even when he'd thought his heart was dead. Even when he'd believed the worst about her, he'd wanted her.

And now, finally, he might get to have her.

He wasn't thinking about tomorrow, wasn't going to imagine what might happen when she saw Justin again or when Justin realised the truth about her. She said she was over him, but she didn't know the whole truth yet.

And, as much as Cooper knew that he should tell her, he couldn't. Not when it might take away this one small chance he had with her.

Tomorrow, all their truths would come out. But until then he was more than happy to keep living the lie.

'A quiet night in sounds perfect to me too.' Leaving his bag beside the counter, he moved closer, towards where she stood by the front door. 'So, would you like the full tour?'

'Sounds great,' she said. Her tongue darted

out across her bottom lip, and Cooper bit back a groan.

The woman was trying to kill him.

Worse, she was killing him and she wasn't even *trying.*

Another step and the space between them disappeared. Dawn dropped her own bag by her feet and leant in when he raised his hands to her waist, resting against another of her mesmerising, brightly coloured tee shirts. The ones he'd been dreaming of stripping off her for almost a week.

Would tonight finally be his chance?

He bent his neck, his lips achingly close to hers. But he couldn't kiss her. Not without being sure.

'Dawn...'

Her eyes were dark when her gaze met his, holding it firm until he couldn't have looked away if he'd tried.

Not that he wanted to try.

'I want this, Cooper,' she said, her voice low and dark. 'I want you. Just once. Just for tonight.'

Just for tonight. That was the deal. Tomorrow belonged to Justin. But tonight...

Tonight Dawn was his.

'Let's start our tour in the bedroom,' he said, and his blood burned as she smiled her agreement.

Okay, so maybe the 'being well rested before seeing Justin again' part of the plan wasn't happening, but Dawn had to admit she felt more relaxed and content than she had in years—even if she might need a nap later to make up for all the lost sleep.

Cooper's apartment faced east and, since they hadn't bothered to close the blinds the night before, sunlight filtered in over them the next morning. Dawn stretched against the expensive cotton sheets, feeling all the kinks and knots in her muscles from the long days in the car giving way under the force of her bone-deep satisfaction.

If all she ever got was one night in Cooper Edwards' arms, at least she'd made the most of every moment of it.

The man himself slumbered on beside her, and she smiled as she watched him sleep. She liked to think he'd remember the night fondly too. Maybe even their whole week together.

He was right, she realised as she sat up, wrapping the top sheet around her naked body. Their trip had felt like a week out of time. Like they were living another life.

But in a few hours they'd be in the Hamptons, where Justin was waiting.

And then her real life started up again. The life in which she'd been abandoned at the altar by yet another man who'd decided she wasn't good enough for him.

Except…she wasn't that Dawn any more. Life on the road might not have been real life, but that didn't mean it hadn't changed her—every bit as much as Cooper said it had changed him. Or maybe…maybe it hadn't. Maybe it had just given her the opportunity to be *herself* again. She'd spent so long trying to be what someone else expected—Justin, her family, every other guy before Justin—that she'd almost forgotten who Dawn was.

But a week on the road with Cooper Edwards had helped her find *her* again.

She knew now that she was more than just the

Dry Run sister. She was more than 'poor Dawn, let down again'. She was worth more than all the sympathy and the pity.

And she knew that she never wanted to wait at the end of another aisle for some guy, or to sit at a romantic restaurant breathlessly waiting for him to get down on one knee.

She wasn't married. So what? She could go out and chase a hundred other dreams—like driving Claudia from coast to coast with the hottest guy she'd ever seen naked—and have a hell of a better time than she ever had waiting to get married.

Yes, she still wanted love. Still wanted someone to love her unconditionally, just the way she was. But she knew now, without a doubt, that Justin wasn't that man.

She liked the Dawn she'd been on her road trip with Justin's best man—but she knew that Justin wouldn't have. He'd have hated the cheap tee shirts with tacky logos, would never have sung along to Elvis on the radio. He'd have wanted consommé in diners that only served waffles, and complained about the beer on tap. And he'd have *hated* Claudia after the first twenty miles.

He'd have loved people seeing him driving such a cool car, but Dawn knew without a doubt that they'd have ditched it for something state-of-the-art with Bluetooth within the first twelve hours.

And, for all that Cooper was supposed to be the workaholic of the two of them, Dawn suspected that Justin wouldn't have been able to stay away from his emails and deals the way Cooper had that week.

Not to mention—although it made her guilty to even think it—the fact that Justin had *never* made her body sing the way Cooper had last night.

Beside her, Cooper stirred, turning under the covers to wrap an arm around her waist and pull her back down against him.

'Good morning, beautiful.' His voice was rough and heavy with sleep, and it made her blood hum with anticipation.

Yes, they had to face Justin today.

But maybe not just yet.

'Good morning,' Dawn said, and kissed him.

CHAPTER FOURTEEN

'GOT EVERYTHING?' COOPER leant against Claudia as Dawn approached with her bag. She'd eventually kicked him out of his own apartment to fetch them breakfast for the road, and so that she could 'actually stand a chance of keeping some clothes on'.

'Think so.' She handed him her holdall and he stowed it in the boot, an action so familiar it was impossible to imagine that this might be the last time he ever did it.

'What about that lacy pink bra I last saw hanging from my bed frame?' It had been a delightful discovery that her lingerie matched the candy colours of her tee shirts.

Dawn's cheeks were tinged with pink. 'Yep, got that.'

'Shame.'

He pulled her in for a kiss before opening the car door for her, enjoying every last second he

could keep her in his arms. He might be re-
solved to give her up at the end of the day, but
that didn't mean he wasn't going to make the
most of the time he had.

They hadn't spoken about what might happen
next but, as he pulled out of the parking garage
and into the sluggish New York traffic, he knew
that it was on her mind as much as his. He could
feel it in the way the silence filled the car. There
was no Elvis on the radio, no ridiculous roadside
attractions to aim for, no twenty questions, I Spy
or even much in the way of conversation at all.

Instead, there was just the two of them staring
out at the road ahead, his hand resting on her leg
and a sense of encroaching dread.

Normally, once Cooper was out of the city,
he started to breathe more easily, the open road
along the coast to the beach house automatically
relaxing him. Today, however, the sight of the
ocean only made him feel even tenser.

He'd avoided thinking about this for as long
as he could, but now the moment was here he
couldn't put it off any longer.

Dawn had to know the truth—that Justin had
left her because he believed a lie. Whether that

would change her feelings, he couldn't predict. But he was fairly sure that Cooper's assurances that Dawn wasn't after the money would go a long way to convincing Justin that it was okay to love her—to marry her, even.

If she still wanted to.

God, what if he'd screwed up his own brother's chance of happiness? How could Justin ever forgive him?

How could Dawn?

No. He might be a despicable human being, but he knew Dawn now. He knew that she had wanted him every bit as much as he had needed her, and if she'd truly loved his brother that couldn't be the case, right?

Maybe, one day, they'd all look back and say that this was all for the best. Somehow. Even if it was impossible to imagine right now.

'Are you okay?' Dawn asked as they approached the familiar road that led to the Edwards family beach house. Had she even been here before? He couldn't remember. Not that it mattered, he supposed.

Nothing much did now.

'I'm fine,' he lied. Then he spotted something

on the side of the road he didn't remember from his last visit and forced a smile. 'Hey, one last stop? For old times' sake?'

He gestured to the new ice-cream parlour, promising the best frozen desserts this side of the Atlantic, and Dawn nodded.

'You and your sweet tooth,' she said fondly. 'I don't know how you're going to go back to salads and vegetable juices after this.'

'Neither do I.' But he wasn't talking about his diet. He meant all of it.

How could he go back to that office and stare at a screen, or play internal politics with the board of directors, when he'd spent a week staring at the open road and the ever-changing landscape of his country? How could he be interested in contracts and deals after he'd had giant polar bears, time capsules and ghost towns?

But most of all how could he go home alone every night, when he'd grown used to having Dawn with him every moment of the day? Just two nights of sleeping in the same bed, and already he couldn't imagine her not being in his arms when he woke up. Just one night of them being together, as close as it was possible to be, and he already couldn't bear to think about never feeling her, touching her that way again.

He should have known that one week, one road trip, with Dawn would never be enough.

He wanted it all. And instead he had to give her back to his brother because that was the honourable thing to do.

And because, however much he wanted it—wanted her in his life forever—he knew that wasn't how it worked for him.

He'd sworn he'd never fall in love that way again, that he'd protect his heart at all costs. And he couldn't break that vow. Not even for Dawn.

Could he?

'Mint choc-chip?' Dawn asked, and Cooper realised he'd been staring at the flavours board for minutes without even seeing them. 'Or do you want to get a couple and share?'

'You pick,' he said, stepping back. 'Get a few for us both to try. I'll…find us a seat.'

He left her debating the merits of honeycomb over rocky road and collapsed into the nearest booth, the smooth plastic seat hard against his back.

He couldn't love her. It had been less than a

week! And, okay, he couldn't remember the last time he'd spent so much time with *anyone*, but this was *Dawn*. His brother's fiancée. The woman who, until a very short time ago, he'd been convinced was only after Justin's money.

But it didn't matter. He knew he'd give her everything he had if it meant she'd stay with him. If she'd help him be the person he'd discovered, out there on the road. The version of himself he liked so much more than the one he had to go back to.

For the first time in his life, he didn't care about the money, about success or family obligations.

He cared about her.

Cared about a woman who loved kooky roadside attractions and hated sugar for breakfast, who couldn't narrow down an ice-cream choice to less than four, it seemed, and who wore cheerful tee shirts and short skirts and had the best legs he'd ever seen. Cared for a woman who listened when he talked of heartbreaks he'd thought he only wanted to ignore, to pack away and never deal with again. Who sang along with Elvis on the radio even when she didn't know the words.

Who kissed him as though she was giving him her whole heart and everything she was.

He loved Dawn the same way that she loved life—with hope, even while expecting to be let down. The way she hoped for happy endings, even after so many romantic disasters.

The way she'd given herself to him, even though she knew it was only for one night.

He loved her.

And he was so far beyond screwed now.

The ice-cream place was nice, but Dawn couldn't help but suspect that Cooper had an ulterior motive for stopping there, so close to the beach house, especially since he hardly even seemed to taste the ice-cream he'd been so desperate to try.

'Which was your favourite?' she asked as they climbed back into Claudia.

'Um, the honeycomb?' he said uncertainly.

'Right.' She hadn't ordered any honeycomb.

So, yes. There was definitely something going on with Cooper. Several times between there and the beach house he opened his mouth, as if about to tell her something, or ask a question, then shut it again without a word.

It was enough to make a girl very nervous indeed. Just in case the idea of facing up to the guy who'd left her at the altar wasn't nerve-racking enough.

Eventually, and just before Dawn's stomach ended up *entirely* in knots, Cooper took one last turn and, suddenly, there it was. The fabled beach house Justin had told her so much about, had shown her photos of, but never actually taken her to.

The white timber fronting glowed in the sunshine, the black shutters framing large windows and matching the gable roofs and the roof of the porch. Out the back, she knew, was a large private pool, and inside would be decorated in perfect beach-house style by whoever Cooper and Justin's mother had paid lavishly to do the job.

It was perfect, and beautiful…and Dawn would far rather have stayed in Claudia than ever go in, if that was okay with everyone.

Except it wasn't.

Cooper stopped the car at the front, then turned to her. 'You ready?'

'No.'

He gave her a small smile. 'You mean we drove

thousands of miles and now you don't even want to go in?'

Put that way, it seemed a little ridiculous. She sighed. 'I suppose I need to get my passport back.'

'Attagirl. Come on. I'll be your wingman.'

The house seemed quiet as they approached, but as Cooper let them in with his key they heard Justin's familiar laugh from the back porch.

Frowning, Cooper moved ahead, dropping Claudia's keys onto a sidetable. Dawn followed, oblivious to the house itself, focused only on that laugh. How could something so familiar sound so alien all of a sudden?

Cooper opened the sliding doors that led out to the pool, then froze. 'Dawn. Maybe you should go back to the car.'

Oh, that wasn't good. Suddenly, the heavy feeling in the pit of her stomach that had plagued her all morning made sense. Whatever this was, it was going to be bad.

But she had to live through it anyway.

Pushing past Cooper, she stepped out onto the porch, feeling the warmth of the day against her skin as she looked out over the pool. There was Justin, his arms wrapped around a slender redhead, his lips on hers, looking happier and more relaxed than she had ever seen him in their months together.

'It's happened again,' she whispered, and Cooper was at her side in an instant. 'He left me and he found true love.'

'He'd better hope it happened that way round.' She glanced up at the thread of fury in Cooper's voice and saw his expression was thunderous. In fact, for someone who'd slept with his brother's fiancée the night before, he looked surprisingly self-righteous, she thought.

But that wasn't the most surprising thing. The part that shocked her most was how angry she *wasn't*.

'Justin!' Cooper yelled, his voice echoing out over the water.

The couple in the pool sprang apart. Justin stared up at them, his eyes wide with shock.

'Cooper? Dawn? Oh, God, Dawn.'

Suddenly, she didn't want to do this. She didn't want to know why she wasn't as good as the woman in his arms. She didn't want to hear that a person couldn't help who they fell in love with, or that everything happens for a reason, or any of the other clichés they all used.

She didn't want to hear any of it.

Turning, she walked back into the beach house. But not before she heard Cooper say, 'Get dried off and get in here *now*, brother. We have things to discuss.'

He shut the screen door behind him and moved across to where she stood, looking at a photo of the two brothers when they'd been much younger, both wearing wetsuits and emerging from the sea. They must have been close once. Dawn wondered what had come between them.

Cooper's hand at her waist made her turn.

'Are you okay?'

'I think so.' She did a quick check for the usual despair and misery that came around this point. Maybe she'd got it all out of her system on the wedding night that wasn't.

Or maybe it just felt different this time because she knew it was for the best.

She sighed. 'I'm not quite sure what I feel. I mean, I'd accepted that Justin had seen the cracks in our relationship before I had—that he'd realised what a mistake it would have been for us to get married. It took me a whole week in a car with you for me to figure it out.' She gave him a crooked grin, but he didn't return it.

'When did you? Figure it out, I mean?'

'I guess it came a bit at a time.' There hadn't been one moment, had there? Just a growing feeling that life as Mrs Justin Edwards might not have suited her as well as she'd assumed, that she'd been jumping into it all too fast. And then the acknowledgment of all the warning signs she'd missed—how she'd had to dress like someone else for Justin, had had to change her habits, her hobbies, what drink she ordered in a restaurant. How she'd never quite fitted in or measured up, never been quite enough.

But, most all, never been truly herself.

Because she'd forgotten who that even was until Cooper had driven across the whole of America with her and helped her figure it out.

She looked up into Cooper's eyes, saw the concern there and knew he was waiting for her to say something more.

'He never saw the real me,' she said slowly. 'Maybe that's why it doesn't hurt so much. He wasn't leaving *me,* but the person I thought he wanted me to be.'

And it wasn't just him, she realised suddenly. It had been all of them.

With Trevor, it had been pretending to like modern art. With Richard, long walks in the countryside where she hadn't even got a pub lunch afterwards. With Harry, she'd had to pretend to love his family the way he did, even though they were vile to her. For Patrick, she'd embraced a love of horse racing she *really* hadn't felt. Even Ewan had wanted her to be more like the ex-girlfriend who'd left him.

Every one of them had wanted her to be someone else.

'I see you.'

Everyone except Cooper.

She'd never bothered to put on an act with him, because she'd never expected anything from him. And somehow he'd given her everything, anyway.

'Dawn, I need to tell you something.' Cooper's words were hurried, his eyes frantic. 'Before Justin gets here. The reason he left—'

But then the screen door opened and Justin

walked in, dressed in chinos and a tee shirt, still rubbing a towel over his wet hair.

'Okay, I'm decent, and Cynthia has gone up to get showered and dressed. Maybe you can tell me what the hell you're both doing here?'

Cooper spun round, anger coursing through his body. 'You want *us* to answer questions? Brother, you're the one who failed to show up for his own wedding, who left me that note saying—well, you know what it said. And now you're here—'

'I don't know what it said.' Dawn's words cut him off as she came to stand beside him, looking between Cooper and her ex-fiancé. 'All he said to me was that he had to give us both our best chance of happiness. I assume, in your case, that meant Cynthia?' Justin at least had the good grace to look a little guilty at that. 'But that's not what he told you, Cooper. Is it? Did you know? Did you know what you were bringing me here to see?'

'No!' God, she thought he'd known Justin had been cheating. He grabbed her arms gently, forcing her to look into his eyes, to see the truth there. 'I swear to you, if I'd known he'd left you for someone else, I'd have told you. After Rachel... You believe that, don't you?'

Dawn gave a slow nod. 'I do. But if it wasn't that...what reason did he give you for leaving?'

And there was the rub. 'He told me he thought you were only marrying him for his money. And...' Hell, but this hurt. 'He knew that would work—that I'd support him and take care of everything—because that's what Rachel did to me.'

'And I told you so before you even married her,' Justin pointed out. 'You didn't listen.'

Cooper ignored him, keeping his gaze fixed on Dawn's, waiting to see the moment she accepted he was telling the truth.

'That's why you hated me so much to start with,' she said. 'You thought I was like your ex-wife.'

'You're nothing like her,' he said fiercely.

'But when did you figure that out?' she asked, her voice dangerously calm. 'Before or after you kissed me?'

Behind them, Justin barked out a laugh. 'Wait! You two are here to berate me for falling for another woman when you've been carrying on together for a whole week behind my back?'

'No.' Dawn turned towards Justin and Cooper could see the fury in every step she took closer to him. Good. She *should* be angry. She *deserved* to be angry.

Maybe this was the closure she really needed.

'I came here for two reasons, Justin. Firstly, because you left with my passport, you utter idiot, so I couldn't go anywhere else. And, secondly, because I needed to know why—why I wasn't good enough for you, why you left me there at the altar. But that one doesn't matter now. Cooper helped me figure it out when he agreed to drive three thousand miles across the country with me.

'It wasn't me that wasn't good enough. *You* weren't deserving enough to see the real me. You wanted me to be a person I'm not, and neither of us would ever have been happy that way in the end. So I'm *glad* you left me at that altar. Because it didn't break me, the way I thought it would. It made me stronger. And, quite frankly, it's none of your damn business what I got up to after that point.'

'None of my business? You're still wearing my ring, Dawn. And you're trying the same tricks on my brother you tried on me!' Justin turned to Cooper. 'I don't know what she's told you, how she's convinced you, but she's just like all the others, Coop. Just like Rachel. She'd do anything to get in with our crowd—do you know, I found a credit card statement just before the wedding? She'd near enough maxed out her cards buying designer clothes, spending cash in fancy bars, all trying to fit in. To be good enough.'

Cooper froze at Justin's words. *Just like Rachel.* But he'd been so sure that Dawn was different. His instincts had screamed at him that she wasn't like the others.

But his instincts had been very, very wrong before.

'That's not how it was!' Dawn protested, but Cooper knew his brother. He knew when he was lying.

And, right now, Justin was telling the truth. And it broke his heart.

'She'd have done anything to marry me,' Justin went on. 'And now she's doing the same thing to you. Being the person she thinks you want her to be so you'll fall for her act. After all, she needs someone else to pick up the tab on those credit cards now, doesn't she?'

Dawn looked up at him, her green eyes wide and panicked, and suddenly he knew for certain that it was all true. Every bit of it.

Of course it was. Because that was all he was to women, wasn't it? A bank account. Why on earth had he let himself believe that Dawn—happy, free and joyful Dawn—would have any interest in a man who barely left the office most days?

He'd been an idiot to think that the last week was anything more than a holiday from reality. Tomorrow, life would go back to normal, and he already knew that Dawn had no interest in living that with him. Hadn't she said just one night?

Would she have pretended to want more, if he'd given her the chance, now that she knew there was no way for her to win Justin back? Maybe. He could almost see it—her sudden change of heart after a night in his bed, needing his comfort after everything with Justin. Suddenly they'd have been talking about living together to save her paying rent, and then it would have been diamond rings, wedding venues and…

And he'd already lived that once. He didn't want it again.

But then Dawn said, 'You know me, Cooper,' her voice low and hard. 'You don't have to listen to him. You know me.'

'I thought I did,' he replied, and watched as the hope in her eyes died.

This. This was the one that was going to break her heart.

'I didn't believe my brother last time, Dawn, and look where that got me.' Divorced, she supposed. And heartbroken. So heartbroken, he wouldn't even risk it again.

Especially not for her. Why would he, when no one else ever had?

'*I* believed your brother, when he told me he loved me, and it got me jilted at the altar,' she pointed out. 'You're going to need a better reason than that.'

He'd told her he saw her. He *knew* her, not whichever act she was putting on today, trying to be the girlfriend or fiancée she though a man wanted her to be.

If Cooper walked away from her, it would be because the *real* her wasn't enough.

And that might ruin her.

'Tell me it's not true.' There was a hint of pleading in his voice, and that surprised her. Cooper Edwards would never beg for anything—she knew that. But here he was anyway, wanting to believe her. 'Tell me you don't have credit cards that need paying off, that you didn't spend money you didn't have trying to fit in with Justin's world, knowing he'd pay it off when you were married.'

Dawn froze. If he'd asked her outright, was she with Justin for his money, the answer would have been easy—no. But that wasn't what he'd asked her.

'I can't,' she admitted. Because that part, at least, was all true. And she'd done it all not to win Justin's money but to win his heart.

And she'd been left with neither.

'Then how does that make you any different from Rachel?' Cooper's voice was flat, the pleading, the hope, all gone.

Dawn shook her head. 'It *is* different. I didn't do those things because I wanted to get my hands on the Edwards family money. But you're never going to believe that, are you?' The realisation chilled her heart. 'It doesn't matter what I say, because you've convinced yourself that the only reason anyone could ever want you is for your money.'

Cooper flinched. 'This isn't about me.'

But it was. She could see it now.

Not caring that Justin was still watching them, Dawn moved closer to Cooper, resting one hand against his chest as she looked up at him, wanting him to look at her the way he had in the beginning. When he'd stared so deep into her soul she thought he might come up again holding all her secrets.

She wanted him to this time. She wanted him to see the heart of her.

She wanted him to understand what she only knew for sure in that moment: she was in love with him.

'It *is* about you,' she whispered. 'About us. You know I don't care about money, and you know, deep down, that the only reason I'd do those things was to find what really mattered to me—true love. I wasn't winning Justin's money, I was winning his heart. But I couldn't, because it wasn't meant for me. He's not my happy ending. I was trying to be the person he needed, the true love he was looking for, but that wasn't me. The Dawn you know…that's the real me. The me that fell in love with you, somewhere in the middle of nowhere on the I-80, when I was least expecting it. When I wasn't trying to be anyone but myself.'

'You can't love me.' His words were a statement, not a question.

'I can't do anything but,' Dawn replied with a sad smile. 'But I know it's not going to make any difference. Not until you believe that you're worth loving for more than your bank account, or your family name.'

Her heart breaking, she stepped away. 'Justin? Courier my stuff to me at the office, okay?' She slipped her engagement ring from her finger and placed it on the table by the photo of the brothers, picking up the keys Cooper had left there. 'Goodbye, boys.'

And with that she walked out of the Edwards'

beach house, climbed into Claudia, her heart aching, and drove away, knowing that this time Cooper wouldn't do a thing to stop her.

CHAPTER FIFTEEN

COOPER WATCHED DAWN walk out of the door and knew in that instant she'd taken his heart with her.

Well, it wasn't as if he'd be using it, anyway. He'd probably hardly notice it was gone, once he got back to work.

'Is she right?' Justin asked, sounding oddly anxious.

Turning to face his brother, Cooper raised his eyebrows. 'Right about what?'

Justin shifted from one foot to the other, looking from the ring on the side table to his brother. 'Do you really think no one could love you for anything but your money?'

'Don't you?' Cooper asked bluntly.

Because that was how it worked. People used love, sex and even friendship to get what they wanted out of the world. And what people wanted most, in Cooper's experience, was exactly what he had: money and power.

Why would anyone want anything else from him?

'I think I might have just made a huge mistake,' Justin said.

Blood pounded in Cooper's ears. 'You want Dawn back.' Hadn't he known it would come to this?

But Justin laughed. 'No, you idiot. And, even if I did, she wouldn't have me.'

'You've got as much money as I have. Why wouldn't she?'

'Because she's in love with you.'

Cooper shook his head and threw himself onto the pale-blue couch his mother thought was calming, but had the most uncomfortable cushions in the world. 'So *now* you believe her motives are pure.'

'I think I might have misunderstood them.' Justin dropped to perch on the coffee table in front of Cooper, his expression sincere. 'I met Cynthia at work, two weeks before the wedding. I told myself that I was imagining the connection between us, that it was just lust or something. Dawn was everything I'd ever wanted in a wife, so what reason did I have to look elsewhere, right? But I couldn't deny the way I felt when I was with Cynthia, and I couldn't avoid her, because we had to work together. And, with every moment that passed, I became more and more certain that she was perfect for me.'

'Why didn't you say something? Call things off earlier?' Cooper asked.

'Because I'm a coward. And I didn't want it to be my fault.'

Cooper huffed a small laugh. That made sense. Justin never had liked taking the blame for anything.

'When I found that credit card statement, I thought about everything you went through with Rachel and I thought…what if this is the same? And maybe I convinced myself it could be, so I had an excuse to not show up at the altar that day.' Justin looked up, his gaze locking with his brother's. 'I don't regret not marrying Dawn. It wasn't meant to be, not the way I'm meant to be with Cynthia.'

They all find their true love and get married within two years.

Dawn's voice echoed in Cooper's head. She was right; it had happened again.

But it wouldn't for him. He was sure of that.

'So, you don't think she's a gold-digger?' Cooper asked.

Justin shook his head. 'And neither do you. Do you?'

'No.' Cooper sighed. 'I've known she couldn't be since almost the day we set out on this road trip, although I tried to convince myself otherwise. I wanted to believe you, brother. And I needed a reason to—' He broke off.

'To keep your hands off her?' Justin guessed.

'Something like that.'

'But the point is, Coop, if she's not after your money, you must have something else she wants.'

'Like?' Because, for the life of him, Cooper couldn't imagine what else he had that was worth a damn.

'Like your heart,' Justin said gently.

But Cooper didn't have that to give. Dawn had already taken it.

And suddenly he wasn't at all so sure he could live without it. Not without holding hers in return.

He jumped to his feet. 'I have to go.'

Laughing, Justin tossed him a set of car keys. 'Her passport's in the glove box. Save me a courier fee.'

'You can spend the savings on our wedding present,' Cooper called back over his shoulder.

Dawn drove and drove. Focussing on the road ahead of her meant that she didn't have to think about everything she'd just walked out on. And, when the thoughts crowded in anyway, she turned Elvis up louder on the radio and let him block out her own pain with songs of his heartache.

Eventually, though, she needed to stop. Even Claudia, the best ride in the country, got a little uncomfortable after a while—and besides, she needed coffee if she was going to do this drive alone.

A familiar sign flashed on the roadside up ahead, and without thinking Dawn turned towards it, parking Claudia alongside Caroline's Diner and trying to forget the man with whom she'd stopped here last.

Inside, everything was just as it had been the

day before, as if her whole world hadn't shifted and quaked since then.

The same waitress who'd served them yesterday brought Dawn a coffee without even being asked, and Dawn sat and sipped it while staring at the menu without reading the words.

Justin had been cheating on her. He'd honestly believed she'd only wanted his money.

And now he'd convinced Cooper of the same.

And Cooper, idiot, believed him. Not because he didn't know Dawn, but because he didn't know *himself.*

Oh, he probably thought he did, but he had no idea. She could sympathise, though. She'd spent long enough being someone she wasn't for other people. She just wished she could have taught Cooper how to break away from that too.

She'd wondered, all through their trip, how to reconcile the Cooper she was getting to know with the one she'd heard stories about. The serious, boring workaholic who was too busy for family, or friends, or love. The business shark who always got the best deal, who protected the family finances and business interests. The protective older brother who didn't approve of Dawn.

None of those people were the Cooper *she* knew. The one he'd been on their road trip.

She wished she could show him the man she'd fallen in love with.

She wished he could see him too.

The bell over the door to the diner rang, but Dawn didn't turn around. There was no one coming for her.

But then the jukebox kicked in and Elvis started playing.

She frowned. Coincidence. It was just that sort of diner.

Then Cooper slid into the seat opposite her, and hope flared in her heart again.

'You were right,' he said.

Dawn sipped her cold coffee. 'About what?'

'Let's say everything, just to be on the safe side.'

'Probably a good idea.'

Cooper sighed. 'I'm sorry. I'm so sorry, Dawn. You know I—'

'I know.' At least, she thought she did. 'You know I'm not after your money.'

'I do. I just… I struggle to see what else you could want.'

'Why?' When it was so blindingly obvious to her, how much more he had to offer.

Running a hand through his hair, Cooper stared across the table at her. 'I told you about Rachel.'

'Just because one woman only wanted you for nefarious reasons, doesn't mean they all will, you know.'

'It wasn't just one.' Cooper looked away out of the window and Dawn felt her heart sink.

'Tell me.' Reaching across, she took his hand in hers and listened.

'When I was twenty-one, and just starting out at the company, my mother brought in this student-placement candidate called Melanie and asked me to show her around. She was gorgeous, and funny, and I played the big guy on campus, showing off for her.'

'So far, so normal. Who wouldn't?'

'Yeah, well. What I didn't know was that she was taking all the company secrets I let slip in an attempt to impress her and passing them on to her boyfriend, who just so happened to work for our competitor.'

Dawn winced. 'Ouch.'

'That's why I should have known better, when Rachel came along. Why I should have listened to Justin when he tried to tell me what she was really like.'

'And why you listened to him this time,' Dawn guessed.

'Exactly.'

She sighed. It wasn't as if she didn't understand his position. Wasn't as though she didn't have fears of her own—that Cooper would turn out to be like every other guy, running off to find his true love the moment he was done with her.

She couldn't know it wouldn't happen. She just had to have faith.

And so did he.

'You told me you don't know what else I could want from you,' she said slowly. 'And I get that in the past people have wanted your money, or your business, or whatever. But to me? That's the least interesting thing about you.'

'Then what is it that *you* want?' Cooper asked.

Dawn smiled. That one was easy. 'I want the man I went on this road trip with. The man who explored weird roadside attractions with me and sang Elvis too loudly with the top down.' Was that so much to ask?

Apparently so. 'The thing is, Dawn...that man doesn't exist. He's...he's like you with Justin. He's me pretending to be someone else, just for a little while. Just for the escape.'

Dawn tilted her head as she looked at him. 'I think you're wrong.'

'You think you know me better than myself?' Cooper asked, eyebrows raised.

How presumptive would she have to be to say yes?

Except she *did.* And he was still wrong.

She took a breath and let it out fast. 'Yes. I'm pretty certain I do.'

'Go on, then. Tell me about myself.' Cooper leaned back in his seat and waited.

The words came without her even having to plan them. A truth she was so sure of she didn't even have to think. She just believed. 'I think, this last week, you were being the person you wanted to be. Free from work and everything else, you got to be yourself, maybe for the first time in years. And I think you liked it.'

'Doesn't change the fact that I have to go

back to normal on Monday morning,' Cooper pointed out.

'It *could*.' He looked at her with confusion, and Dawn sighed. 'I spent months trying to be the woman I thought Justin wanted, right? I was playing a part. But, with you, I was myself. And I think you're looking at it the wrong way round. The person you're going back to when you walk into the office on Monday…that's the act. That's you being who you think you need to be. But you don't. You could be *my* Cooper, all the time.'

'Yours, huh?' Cooper gave her a small smirk.

Dawn stood her ground. This wasn't a joke. This was their future. Possibly. 'If you wanted.'

And he *did* want. She could see it in his eyes. The only question was whether he'd let himself have it. 'And if I do? What happens now?'

Wasn't that the million-dollar question? Dawn sighed, swirling the last of her coffee around in her cup while she considered her answer.

Love had always been easy for her. It was making it last she'd struggled with. And this, she knew, was her best chance. She had to do this right, and she had to do it her way. As herself.

'I have to go back to California,' she said eventually. 'I have a job to get back to. I have to check on my family, distribute Buffalo Bill keyrings before they all fly home. I have to sort out my life, my*self*. Figure out how to live as me again, before I can do anything else.'

'And us?' Cooper asked. 'What happens there?'

She looked up at him, smiling sadly. 'I think you need to do the same thing. I think you need to go figure out the Cooper you want to be, in the real world, not just on the road. And then...'

'And then we can try,' Cooper finished for her. 'See who we are *together*.'

'Exactly,' Dawn said, relieved that he seemed to get it.

She didn't want to leave him. But she needed to know that she'd be able to stay—and so would he. Needed to know who she was on her own, before she let anyone else in again. And just in case, once she was gone, Cooper did what everyone else had done and found what he was really looking for—and that it wasn't her.

It was a risk, but one she knew she had to take.

Maybe she wouldn't find her happy-ever-after with Cooper. But she wanted to give it her best shot. As herself.

Cooper lifted her hand from the table. 'I've got your passport in the car. I'll drive you to the airport in Claudia. Justin can get a ride out here and pick up his car himself.'

'Eager to get rid of me?' she asked.

'Eager to get you back again.' He frowned. 'Should we set a date? A place?'

Dawn considered. 'Three months.' If she couldn't get things together in that amount of time, she probably never would. 'You can pick the place.'

Cooper's smile made her feel a little nervous. 'I'll let you know,' he promised.

Dawn smiled back, already knowing that these were going to be the hardest and longest three months of her life.

Three months later

Kansas in November was cooler than Cooper had imagined it would be. Still, if everything went to plan, things should be warming up any time now.

As long as Dawn showed up.

It had been a long three months. Sure, they'd texted most days, and called from time to time, but the process of extracting themselves from the lives they'd been living for others, and finding the ones they wanted to live for themselves, had taken time and energy.

Cooper had started small. Listening to Elvis in his office. Eating a burger for lunch now and then. Finding the quirkiest and weirdest New York attractions and visiting them. He'd started choosing his own clothes—ones he liked, rather than ones that matched what everyone else wore at the office.

Next, he'd upped his game by actually taking weekends. Of course, he'd struggled to fill them alone, but it turned out that some of his colleagues could actually become friends, if he gave them the chance, so he'd tagged along on nights out, trips to sports events and even a birthday party or two.

It all felt a little empty without Dawn, but even then he was happier than he'd been in years—except that week on the road with her.

His biggest step, though, had been with the board of directors. It had taken some convincing, but between Justin and him they'd managed it—and, suddenly, Cooper's whole life opened up with possibilities. Which was what led him here, to Kansas, in November.

Standing beside the world's biggest ball of twine with a diamond ring in his pocket.

'That is one *big* ball of twine.'

Cooper spun at the sound of her voice, moving towards her even before he saw her. When he did, he stopped and just drank in the image.

She had her hair up, bouncing in a high ponytail that hit between her shoulder blades. Her bright pink lipstick matched her woollen coat, and her smile lit up his heart.

'You came,' he said, still amazed at how beautiful she was.

'You think I'd miss the world's biggest ball of twine? Never.' Stepping closer, she braced a hand on his chest and stood on tiptoes to press a kiss to his mouth. 'Besides, I missed *you* too much.'

'I missed you too,' he murmured back. 'So much.'

'So, I have news,' Dawn said.

'So do I.' News he really, really hoped she'd like.

'I quit my job,' Dawn said. 'Only, not really.'

'That makes no sense.'

She grinned. 'I know. The thing is, I loved doing the marketing and promo side of my work, but working with the same products all the time... it got a little dull. So I decided to go freelance, and my company hired me on the spot to keep doing what I'm doing, only for more money. Plus I get to take on other clients, too, and I can work from anywhere I want in the world.'

'That sounds...perfect.' And it happened to fit in perfectly with his plans too.

'What's your news?'

'Justin and I decided to change the structure of the business,' Cooper said, remembering his brother's smile when he'd suggested it. 'He's taking over a lot of the stuff I used to do—which, since Cynthia wanted to move to New York anyway, is pretty much perfect for them.'

'So what will you be doing?' Dawn asked, a small frown in the middle of her forehead.

'Basically? Whatever the hell I want.'

She laughed. 'You don't take half-measures when it comes to designing your ideal life, do you?'

'Why should I?' Cooper asked. 'The deal is

that the business will utilise me in a consultant capacity—using my knowledge of the business and the market to troubleshoot wherever I'm needed. It means more time travelling, visiting different sites, different places.'

'Sounds like you'll be on the road a lot.'

'Which is why I bought Claudia,' he admitted. 'And this.' He pulled the ring from his pocket and held his breath.

'You bought Claudia?' Dawn asked, still caught up on the first part of his sentence. 'The most impractical car in existence who only plays Elvis?'

'You love that car. I'm also rather hoping you might like the ring.'

Her eyes widened as she finally focussed on the diamond in his hand. 'You want to marry me?'

'I want to spend my life with you,' he corrected. 'On the road, at home, everywhere. I want to be with you. Everything else is negotiable.'

'Except for Claudia.'

'Hell, yes, we're definitely keeping Claudia.'

'I can live with that.' Dawn finally raised her

gaze from the ring to his eyes, and his breath caught at the hope and love he saw there.

'You haven't said yes yet,' he pointed out.

She smiled. 'You already know my answer.'

'I'd still like to hear it.'

Carefully, Dawn took the ring from his hand and placed it on her ring finger. 'Yes, Cooper Edwards. I'll go anywhere and everywhere with you. For ever.'

'That's all I'll ever need,' Cooper said. 'Well, that and doughnuts for breakfast.'

Dawn laughed, and he kissed her, knowing their adventure together was only just beginning.

* * * * *

LET'S TALK

Romance

For exclusive extracts, competitions
and special offers, find us online:

f facebook.com/millsandboon

⟲ @millsandboonuk

🐦 @millsandboon

Or get in touch on 0844 844 1351*

For all the latest titles coming soon,
visit millsandboon.co.uk/nextmonth

Want even more
ROMANCE?

Join our bookclub today!

'Mills & Boon books, the perfect way to escape for an hour or so.'

Miss W. Dyer

'Excellent service, promptly delivered and very good subscription choices.'

Miss A. Pearson

'You get fantastic special offers and the chance to get books before they hit the shops'

Mrs V. Hall

Visit millsandbook.co.uk/Bookclub and save on brand new books.

MILLS & BOON